To
M[...]

thanks for all your
support

Hope that you enjoy
this light & airy tale

Don't have nightmares!

All my love
Wayne xxx
x

Wayne Sharrocks was born in the London Borough of Camden. After attending college he embarked on a career within animal welfare before returning to his passion for writing.

He now lives in the picturesque village of Blo Norton, situated on the Norfolk/Suffolk border, and is enjoying his new profession as an author of psychological thrillers.

Dominion is his second novel, with the third already in the pipeline for future release.

In his spare time he enjoys art & design and is still a keen supporter of a number of animal welfare charities.

Books by the same author

Redemption
ISBN 1 84386 254 9

DOMINION

Wayne Sharrocks

DOMINION

Vanguard Press

VANGUARD PAPERBACK

© Copyright 2007
Wayne Sharrocks

The right of Wayne Sharrocks to be identified as author of this work has been asserted by him in accordance with the Copyright, Designs and Patents Act 1988.

All Rights Reserved

No reproduction, copy or transmission of this publication may be made without written permission.
No paragraph of this publication may be reproduced, copied or transmitted save with the written permission of the publisher, or in accordance with the provisions of the Copyright Act 1956 (as amended).

Any person who commits any unauthorised act in relation to this publication may be liable to criminal prosecution and civil claims for damages.

A CIP catalogue record for this title is available from the British Library.

ISBN 978 1 84386 385 4

*Vanguard Press is an imprint of
Pegasus Elliot MacKenzie Publishers Ltd.*
www.pegasuspublishers.com

First Published in 2007

**Vanguard Press
Sheraton House Castle Park
Cambridge England**

Printed & Bound in Great Britain

DEDICATION

This book is dedicated to the memory of Mick Clark
Who recently passed over from this realm.
A true friend and a
great supporter throughout my career.
You are greatly missed.

ACKNOWLEDGENTS

I would like to convey my sincere gratitude to all those who have supported me both personally and professionally; in particular Shaz Davey, Mark Earl, Rosie, Spider, Rachel Hives, Jenny Oliver, Ross Maclaren, Peter Casburn, Ian Robertson, Nickie & Rob, Magda, Kelly (Spike), Jill Garratt, Emma Jones, Ed & Val Gascoyne, Michelle Courtney, Chris & Elaine Astridge, Petra Barnby, Anthony Bond, Sandra Barber, David Newstead, Brenda Young and all at Pegasus who have allowed me the opportunity to reach out and touch kindred spirits from around the globe. Many thanks.

PROLOGUE

Sat hunched within the dark recess Karl Connor felt as small and vulnerable as a china doll. As what seemed like hours passed he could feel the welts from the cigarette burns rising up on his body, smarting, searing…

His body still hissed from the pain of his mother's nails gouging his young and tender flesh. As dread washed through him, how he longed for a shining light in the great dark loneliness of human existence.

Terror began with the fact that he could hardly move. His mind wrestled with some unbalanced nightmare, whilst his body ached with cramps and knots in his muscles. The cupboard under the stairs was no more than three feet long, roughly the same in height and was crammed full of assorted bric-a-brac (a vivid testimony to his mother's car-boot compulsion).

As his panic escalated inside of him, all his desires diminished to just the need to move, a desperate, overwhelming need to free himself from the dark and cramped conditions that he now found himself trapped within. As his mind fractured he tried to scream but found that he could not even speak. The unbearable stress shattered his logic to pieces, finally breaking him from reality as thoughts like moths fluttered through his mind, seeking light in his darkness.

The punishment was as if a tourniquet around his neck, strangling the life from him. His pallor ghostly, he began to writhe and squirm as his shoulders began to shake. His grief extensive enough to bring down an empire. As the vast waiting silence dragged him down like exhausted sleep, his wanting – longing to be freed – filled the space oppressively.

Crippled by fear he was aware of the darkness sucking him down.

Although he had long since managed to spit out the rag that was stuffed into his mouth to stifle his earlier protestations, his breath was still very shallow, trapped by the dull suffocating heat of the blackness that had encroached upon him. He found that his palms were sweating. He had gnawed at his knuckles until they bled, sucking at the warm blood that flowed from them as if it were comforting nectar. Recoiling, his mind snatched feebly at passing thoughts whilst above him, he could hear the sound of the splintering wood and the creaking floorboards. He could hear his mother's gin soaked voice echoing as she descended the wooden staircase, her rage biting deep.

'Filthy, dirty boy, I told you he wasn't right, he is the devil's child. I should have had him aborted when I had the chance…'

Moments later he heard the catch being slid from the lock and the cupboard door sprang open, battering his eyes with light.

Springing back from the sudden brilliance, he flinched as the light scolded his vision, momentarily dazzling him.

A torch shone in his eyes but all he could see was the glare, burning his eyes and dragging him still further into his mother's alcohol fuelled nightmare.

Her voice now seemed distant and slurred as she brandished the huge torch at him. Under the skin on the back of his neck, ticks of apprehension still burrowed and twitched, but heart pounding he unfurled from the fetal position that he had been forced into and achingly crawled out from the cupboard. His muscles and limbs screamed with every movement and the abrupt definition of sight stung his eyes, whilst his nerves were shredded and crippled by his own deceiving mind.

His face had whitened and as he turned his head to look at his mother, his expression was desperate and pleading.

Believing that to be the end of the punishment he began to apologize, even though he sensed that he had done nothing wrong. As he spoke, there was a tremor in his voice, fragility, not pain so much as emotional distress. The hardness of her heart frightened him. He had taken two faltering steps before he was doubled over, as if a hook had caught his stomach, knocking the air from him. The world with all its cruelty and violence had now become too strange for him to fully comprehend, and as the large torch lay broken in pieces upon the threadbare carpet, he gazed meekly up at his mother, into a face set with thunder and into eyes as cold as ice.

His face took on a crumbling almost collapsed look before he let out a cry of sheerest childlike terror, but as he tried to kid himself into believing that life had a purpose worthy of his struggle he knew deep down that he would be made to pay further for his actions…

CHAPTER 1

CONTINUANCE

Eventually arriving home after spending the last few hours caught up amongst the seemingly endless tube delays and cancellations, Jackie Newell could not wait to hit the shower and wash the stains of the day from her tense and fatigued body. She just needed to make a quick phone call to the office first and then the warm invigorating jets of water could work their never ending magic on her stiff and aching muscles. She fumbled absently inside her handbag for the front door key, taking care not to spill the shopping that was currently wedged precariously in the crook of her left arm. Eventually retrieving the key, she proceeded to slide it into the lock whilst gently easing the door open with her elbow. Keeping it ajar with her foot, she bent down to place the box of groceries onto the wooden hall table. She then stooped to gather the post and the milk from the doorstep. Glancing down at the handful of brown windowed envelopes, visions of the enclosed bold red writing came to the forefront of her mind. Business had been slow for a while now and as a result she had been feeding the bills into the mouth of her paper shredder as if it were a hungry chick.

Her train of thought was suddenly disturbed as she heard a heavy footfall and witnessed a dark shadow fall across her path. She went to look up but as she did so she felt a gloved hand clasp her mouth tightly shut. She could taste the beaten leather and at that moment she saw the glint of steel as a knife flashed across her eye line. She froze in terror as she was bundled through the open door and into the narrow cluttered hallway. She heard the foreboding sound of the front door slam decisively shut behind them. She knew instantly what fate awaited her.

Before she could cry out for help or plead for mercy, she heard the knife click shut and felt the attackers hands clamp tightly around her neck. She longed to scream but no sound would come. She gasped for air, whilst kicking out desperately, her hands flailing wildly, trying to scratch and claw at her assailant. It was all to be to no avail, as she felt herself becoming weaker as her assailant grew stronger. As a hot trickle of urine ran down her leg, she noted that her breath was becoming weak and rasping as she gulped for air. Desperately her hands flew to her throat as she felt her strength and life cruelly ebbing away from her. Her eyes were bright with tears as a galaxy of tobacco smelling dust hung suspended in the air above her, having been reluctantly disturbed by the struggling and twisted forms below.

Her face was squeezed tight with pain but her assailant's grip remained unyielding. He was just too strong and too powerful to fight off and the tears were now streaming down her face, coating her lips with the taste of salt before dropping off of her delicate chin and onto the increasingly threadbare carpet below. Although she could not see his ever-present smirk she could feel his cold hateful stare on the back of her neck.

Her mouth was twisted in a scream never voiced, whilst her eyes grew wide, welling with terminal tears.

She had long since resigned herself to her fate before all light was extinguished and her world turned black…

Tossing the sweat soaked body down he allowed himself a satisfied grin. In the embrace of death, the heightened flow of adrenaline was coursing through his blood causing his heart to hammer wildly inside his chest and his penis to stand to attention. There was nothing like experiencing the thrill of life being drained away. His determination and will had not yet deserted him, and if anything, his extermination of the loathsome insects had now reached clinical precision. Quite why they had all fought so hard and shown such a desperate will to live was a complete mystery to him.

The world was intensely cruel, so surely they should have been grateful to him for their merciful release from this mortal coil? It baffled him more than angered him…the last one had even dug her fingers into him so hard that most of her fingernails had broken off. Surely that had just given her more pain than it had been necessary to suffer? At that unconscious thought he felt a slight tickle of excitement run through his loins. He knew that he was doing them a service as at least in death they would not be treated the way that they had in life, left alone and forgotten. He had always known that he would be lost without his mission…it was his calling, what he was put on this earth to do. Separating the wheat from the chaff, what could be more important?

His bitterness was a fulcrum and his inner rage a reason to hate the world.

For a minute he just crouched in silence, savouring the thrill of the kill. He then straightened himself up and stepping over the body, strode purposefully across the living room to turn on the radio to cover any noise that would follow…

CHAPTER 2

DEADLOCK

Due to the gridlocked traffic Detective Inspector Ross had arrived late at the crime scene. As he pulled up to the kerbside of the tree lined avenue he looked up through the windscreen and watched as a cadaver, on a wheeled stretcher covered in a thin white body bag with black straps, was loaded unceremoniously into the back of the coroner's black van.

The whizzing sound of a police helicopter intensified in the distance, rapidly growing louder, shaking him from his stupor.

Previously deep in thought, he now caught sight of his reflection in the rear view mirror and could see that his face had turned as white as the swollen moon above. He took a moment to compose himself before he swung the driver's door open. He raised his hand in a vague wave to acknowledge the two body movers from the coroner's office as they turned with a darting urgency from the rear of the van. Still encased in their white coveralls, they mirrored his gesture before walking quickly towards the front of their vehicle.

Detective Inspector Ross remained watching as they pulled away from the kerb and set off into the traffic. He then glanced over at the house, which was cordoned off by fluorescent yellow crime scene tape that fluttered in the breeze like ribbons from a maypole. An assorted throng of media types and rubbernecks, some of whom were now attempting to take photographs on their mobile phones, had already assembled at the scene and looked on like a pack of baying jackals only just being kept at bay by the increasingly thin blue line.

He blew out a noisy sigh as he continued to look out of the car window at the unfurling scene.

He was less than thrilled to get a call like this on what so far had been his first day off in little over a month, especially as he sensed that his days at the helm of the investigation were numbered and such a public fall from grace would all but finish his previously fast-track career. At that thought his jaw tightened and he felt a slight tickle of electric current go down the back of his neck, bringing the hairs there to attention. A knot of anxious tension gripped his stomach, a subconscious fear of failure.

His palms shuddered, shivered, as he trembled with anxiety.

He was back in the entanglement of guilt he forever struggled to be free of.

He willed himself to relax but as his body was stiff and his muscles ached from lack of sleep his mind had no intention of obeying him. He took a deep breath and swept his hand through his steel grey hair so that most of it fell back into place, whilst the wind took the other rogue strands so that they resembled dancing marionettes.

Ross removed his black wool sport coat and threw it onto the passenger seat before undoing his cuffs and rolling up his sleeves, a display that was intended to state to onlookers that he was getting ready for business.

After fighting his way through the escalating crowd, which combined the concerned, the curious and the ghoulish, he flashed his warrant card before ducking under the police tape to enter the crime scene.

As he reluctantly breathed in the chill of the evening, he stared over at the house. It looked unkempt, the garden untended, neglected even. As he walked towards it, the press continued to bombard him with queries, some pleadingly, others rudely, but he ignored them all. He had already braced himself for the media storm, which now inevitably followed every new victim. As he stepped inside the house he could still hear their voices being carried away by the wind, muttering and complaining. Due to the current atmosphere of fierce criticism, several patrol cars sat in front of the house, protecting the scene. Behind them he could see that the scenes of crime officers were already busy measuring and taking relevant samples, hoping that it would yield a harvest of vital information. The fingerprint guys stood to one side, as they had to wait until late on in the scientific process as the powders and chemicals they used could possibly contaminate other evidence finds.

Detective Sergeant Armstrong, who was fast approaching middle age and plagued by thinning hair, was already in the premises and was deep in conversation with a couple of uniformed officers who had been the first ones to arrive at the scene after the emergency call had been received. Huddled together, their hoarse whispers were barely audible above the background cacophony of noise that was filtering in from the assorted rabble outside.

Detective Inspector Ross approached them, eager to be filled in on the story so far, his voice cracking from disuse.

"Is it like the others?"

"Yeah, seems so governor, it looks to be the same modus operandi."

Detective Inspector Ross had feared that would be his response and felt a slight quiver move through his body.

His voice had scarcely changed, but a new alertness coloured it, a shade of wariness.

"Do we have a name for her yet?"

Detective Sergeant Armstrong flipped open his notepad, checking his notations, attempting to decipher his scrawl.

Finally he cast his eyes upward to meet Detective Inspector Ross's.

"Yes governor, a Miss Jackie Newell. A neighbour found her and has given us a positive identification. Next of kin have been notified, thankfully by us before they got to see the gruesome details of their daughter's demise splashed all over the early evening news."

"Have any witnesses come forward yet?"

"No, governor, people round here are like the three wise monkeys: See no evil, hear no evil and speak no evil. It must be a slow day for the media as well as I've been getting more 'what's happening' calls than incoming information from the general public."

Whilst uniformed officers milled around, waiting for orders, the background cacophony of noise was rising again; obviously the reporters who were currently huddled in packs were eagerly awaiting a press release, but they would be made to wait on.

In Detective Inspector Ross's absence Detective Sergeant Armstrong had assumed the role of team leader and ensured security at the crime scene so as not to taint any possible trace evidence. As well as weathering the initial blizzard of press and media attention, he had also conducted the initial walk-through and ensured that the photographer, scenes of crime officers and medical examiner had all been notified and were subsequently present at the scene.

A detailed and thorough search was now being conducted and a catalogue of physical evidence, in the way of sample fibres, hairs and bodily fluids was being collected and recorded, whilst the cordoned off area had been meticulously photographed.

Angled lights from electric torches now shone on surfaces currently being dusted with powder, hoping to pick up latent prints. Any prints found were being developed and then lifted with transparent tape. Each piece of tape was then being stuck onto a piece of white card and deposited into the evidence case to await analysis by the crime lab technician, after an elimination set of fingerprints had been taken later from the victim.

Scenes of crime officers and the photographer who were all encased in disposable white jumpsuits, masks, booties, head cover and latex gloves were now packing up to depart, having bagged, tagged, photographed and sealed all the evidence containers.

Detective Inspector Ross approached them cautiously.

"Did he leave much to go on this time?"

"Minimal. It looks like the same guy but we will know more when we get the laboratory results back. Obviously we will let you know as soon as we hear anything. We have finished here now, so it is your crime scene."

As Detective Inspector Ross grunted a response with a minimum of enthusiasm, his eyes drifted to the medical examiner, who was stood propped against the far wall, orating into his Dictaphone, which he gripped in his hand proudly as if it were a cherished prize. Ross nodded an acknowledgement to him but chose to speak to him later as he appeared to be in full oratory flow, his voice crisp and now without even a hint of the strong regional accent with which he had communicated in his younger days.

Detective Inspector Ross could never understand why people disinherited their roots quite so easily.

Turning back to Detective Inspector Armstrong and the two uniformed officers, he conveyed his orders that he wanted the neighbourhood canvassed in an attempt to search out witnesses, including those who may not know that they have useful information about the crime currently under investigation. The same went for the onlookers at the scene, who he noted had now swelled to double their original figure, eager to be part of the unfurling drama, their own version of 'reality television'. Obviously there was nothing too riveting on the television tonight or else their video recorders were now eagerly sapping the power from the local electricity grid.

As the officers and the evidence recovery team began departing the premises Detective Inspector Ross stood deep in thought, his digits raised into a steeple that just touched his lip as if subconsciously offering a silent prayer for help.

Depressed and bitter, he was snapped out of his musings by a rivulet of perspiration that dropped from his forehead, landing on his nose with a splash.

Looking outside the perimeter he noted that the media encampment was becoming increasingly raucous, as the clamour for statements intensified. The press had been swarming all over the case like hornets, and as much as he loathed the media in all their forms, he knew that for as long as he was directing the investigation a co-operative spirit would need to be harnessed and maintained.

The news of this latest murder had cut through the air like an arrow and landed like a bombshell, hence the media were waiting en masse for an interview.

The anger he was previously feeling was momentarily gone but only to be replaced by sadness. Flashbacks from the previous murders caused a wave of depression to wash over him, causing his body to slightly shiver as if it were suddenly being immersed in ice.

Frustrated, angered and sorely confused, he was eager to find a pattern, a trail of circumstances as the mounting questions made him feel colder and lonelier than ever before. The pieces of the jigsaw just did not fit together and he knew that after an eight-month investigation and now six victims he was no nearer finding the killer than he had been on the very first day.

As he eyed the room he noted that inside one of the panes of glass in the downstairs window was pasted an orange sticker that stated the area was part of the local neighbourhood watch scheme. If the circumstances had not been quite so horrific he may have afforded himself a wry grin at the irony of there being no witnesses to the crime.

As he rubbed his forehead with his palm anyone viewing him would have noted that his face was heavy with regret, his eyes looked fatigued and weary, whilst his forehead was lined with worry. He felt weighed down by weariness and even his heavy eyebrows had started to grey over in recent weeks so that they now resembled geriatric caterpillars.

As if jealous that his mind was getting all the attention his stomach suddenly growled with hunger. He had grabbed a sandwich from a local garage on the way to the incident, but had found that he could not eat much of it, as the bread had tasted stale and the cheese rubbery. He had even checked the sell by date on the packaging but in his experience they tended to be as reliable as a milometer on a second hand car.

He fell silent for a while, his mind dipping into regret and resignation as he drew a breath so painful that it felt like he was choking. His face clouded with doubt as he sucked in air through his teeth, before closing his eyes briefly, trying to hold his emotions in check. Eight months of restless nights had taken their toll as revelation had eluded him.

He wriggled his broad shoulders in a bid to work out the tension and massaged the cramp from his thighs before raising himself up ramrod straight, so that his six foot two inch frame seemingly filled the room. As he eyed the reception area it struck him that it was once probably homely and welcoming but now it appeared chilly and unpleasant, a place where secrets hung in the air like dust.

As he looked around he noted that the medical examiner had now finished his notations and was just standing, observing the crime scene. He approached him more out of professional courtesy than need, as the manner of death left little debate.

The medical examiner reconfirmed what Ross already suspected. He appeared to have reached an impasse and there seemed no way forward and no more leads to follow.

Although spinning in his own emotional turmoil, he could sense the spectre of failure taking shape in everyone's mind.

As he revisited the previous murder scenes in his mind's eye, he was back in the entanglement of the guilt that he forever struggled to be free of, images that haunted his sleep.

Despite the expression of resolve on his face, the reality was that perhaps he would never know the reasons behind the murderous rampage.

He drew a deep breath, before exhaling with a shudder.

As Detective Sergeant Armstrong appeared from the shadows of the hallway, looking equally discouraged and exhausted, having returned from pursuing enquiries locally, Detective Inspector Ross felt the sense of dread once again rising from within him.

Lost in worried thought, he bristled a little, as he knew that he was in the clutches of a seemingly motiveless murderer. His career was going down the drain and he sensed that even belonging to the right lodge could not save him this time. He desperately needed to establish a pattern, a common connection that may prevent further casualties. He had screwed up once; he could not afford to let it happen again.

The missing pieces of the puzzle, however, greatly bothered him.

The cases had proved to be the most complex of his career and he felt as if he had reached an impasse. There seemed no way forwards and no more unexplored routes to go along.

Perhaps the real murderer had even framed his original suspect to distract the police enquiry. That would fit, he thought…

He forced the idea out of his mind almost as soon as it had entered as he knew deep down that he was now just clutching at straws.

As he made his excuses to leave, he exited the front door, shutting it firmly behind him with a thud that sounded like a guillotine blade coming down. He just hoped that it would not prove to be an ironic epitaph to his career.

CHAPTER 3

ANGEL OF DEATH

Karl Connor awoke slowly to find himself spread-eagled within his king-size bed. He drank in the space and the solitude that was afforded to him as he had learnt a long time ago to believe in nothing and no one. Utter indifference was his friend and his consolation. When most people opened their mouths, out came a family of lies, hence he felt that life was a charade, the characters and scenery changed but the general text never altered. As love was always over the next morning, no company compared to his own, of that he did not have any doubt. He let the thought glide through his mind as if it were a silk kite, floating and distant upon the summer air.

Reaching over for the glass of crystal-clear water (that sat perched precariously upon the bedside cabinet) he sipped gingerly, eager to soothe his parched and dry throat but wary of the lacerations that currently adorned his neck as if tribal markings. Swallowing, he sat up and let his gaze drift over the bedroom walls of his opulent abode, inwardly grinning at the ornaments smiling down on him as if he and they were old friends.

His home had had the kind of facelift that Hollywood A-listers could only dream about...

He fumbled for the switch on the bedside lamp and turned it on before reaching for his black Thai silk dressing gown, which was hanging limply from the bedpost. Slipping it over his bare torso he arose slowly and ambled across the room towards the bedroom window. For a long time he just stood there frozen, pressed against the partially drawn curtains, being framed by the dim light from the headlight beams of passing traffic. The windows shook slightly as a heavy goods vehicle went by.

The room itself although tastefully and exquisitely decorated (but without the seemingly obligatory flowers, cushions or cuddle toys) would probably be considered relatively sparse by modern day standards. A huge Colonial four poster bed with barley twist columns and detailed carving dominated the room and was positioned opposite a full length Malaysian hardwood mirror and adjacent to a fine Gothic style rosewood wardrobe, all of which he had salvaged from a Notting Hill market vendor whose ignorance of such fine pieces had bordered on incompetence.

Reaching up to pull the vintage dark blue velvet curtains apart, the room was suddenly flooded with harsh yellow sunlight like the flames of an intense fire. The brightness momentarily hurt his eyes before he managed to turn, catching his reflection trapped within the huge mirror. Trim and athletic in stature, he noted that his blond hair shone in the light whilst his complexion positively glowed with good health. He knew that with his piercing aquamarine eyes, short nose and full lips, others considered him a handsome man. For that he would be eternally grateful, as his good looks had always made it easier for him to gain favour with the opposite sex. Turning he retreated to switch off his bedside lamp before heading towards the bathroom to shower, shave and dress. Whilst the shower's warm jets of water worked their magic on his taut skin, easing and relaxing his aching muscles, his mind wandered to a fleeting moment of contentment. The effect was soothing and he was now eager to enter the summer stillness of the early morning to begin the adventures that the new day on his hunting ground may hold...

When he finally re-emerged from the bathroom he was clad in a crisp white cotton shirt, black velvet blazer and pleated black cotton trousers... today's costume of choice in the world's play of innocence and danger.

He had inherited a great deal of money, due to both of his parents succumbing to a dreadful accident, so he did not need to endure the tedium of employment or mimic any human emotion. From a very young age, he knew that a dangerous passion had always welled within him but he had always managed to keep it concealed from the outside world. The closest anyone had come to threaten his existence had been during the inquest into his parents' sad demise.

There had been malicious whispers and senseless chatter for a while but his play at wide-eyed innocence had soon nailed the lid shut on any formal charges ever being brought.

From youth he had always had the strangest of dreams and since his parents' early passing he had found that the dreams and his own reality had now merged to become one, his head now positively swimming with dark obsessions and twisted fantasies, his vision of importance and power ever escalating. From childhood he'd had no time for people – as much like politicians – they were either corrupt or incompetent, good ones as rare as white taxi drivers in London. He knew early that life was a struggle but now he could almost feel the mask of sanity beginning to slip.

Exiting his front door he walked languidly into the early morning sunlight. As it was already warm and without a breath of wind in the air he decided to leave his car and walked deliberately through the neighbourhood, viewing everything, his mind pulling on the thread of expectation...his pleasure opening up to him as if he were an expectant child.

The most shocking thing about that hour was the silence.

The streets were empty and he managed to ignore the infrequent passing traffic as in his solitary happiness, the silence and emptiness of the world was manna from heaven. It was in these private moments when he was unguarded, that he saw everything with exaggerated clarity, which was a blessed relief from his tainted past. He enjoyed the accessibility and the anonymity that the capital provided.

A faint smile floated across his mouth.

Whilst he moved through the air with careful pleasure, his falling shadow formed a dark score across the sunlit flagstones, as if it were an apology for his trespass.

The morning was still and warm and heat shimmered off the paving stones.

Chimneys with aerials spiraled up from steep red tiled roofs to form crosses against the skyline. In front of the houses, lawns formed a long sweep of green, interrupted only by the odd gravel pathway, the complete composition balanced and restful, as radiant as angels.

The sun came out from behind a cloud, forcing him to squint, and feeling, as he did so, tight lines forming around the corners of his eyes.

As he strode he noticed a woman crossing the road up ahead of him. His surprise at seeing her was disproportionate to the event but he had been enjoying the solitude that had been afforded to him. She was still some distance away but he could see that she walked with an air of self-assurance and self-confidence.

From what he could make out, she was attired in a long dark printed flowing skirt and lightly patterned blouse, a messy assemblage that sadly deflected attention away from her beautifully long tawny hair. Due to her attire, he got the feeling that there was something utterly disorganized about her but it fed his unabashed curiosity. The unhappiness he had known in his life he guarded with a composure that was often mistaken as hardness of manner, but for some reason he suddenly felt perplexed by her arrival. Pale as a spirit, there was something strangely familiar in her features and demeanor, and as he studied her, he was filled with a cold vague panic. Karl blinked. He felt that his own defences were now weakening and his previous comfortable state was scarcely traceable. He wondered if he should turn on his heels to avoid the impending social contact and the dire distress that now seemed somehow inevitable. A vision formed in his mind, as vivid as the fires of hell. A small boy was curled up in a ball, body squirming and thrashing, writhing and arching up, as a belt flailed wildly at him, forming welts where it landed. Frozen in fear, a chill climbed the ladder of his spine, vertebra by vertebra. Inside he was pleading for it all to stop but although he longed to scream until his throat tore apart, when he opened his mouth to shriek his tongue and lips quivered convulsively without issuing a sound. His arteries throbbed in his neck and temple as the nausea grew worse.

Lost within his mind, he inadvertently stepped off the pavement into the path of an oncoming lorry, whose blaring horn jarred him from his trance, startling him back to reality. Terrified he jumped back onto the pavement before clamping his hands to his body, certain that he would find his flesh ripped and bleeding, but he was relieved to discover that he was not injured, his flesh was intact and that the events had just been a flashback, stills from a seemingly not unforgotten past.

Teetering on the edge of his own sanity, he momentarily closed his eyes and tried to gather his unravelled nerves into a tight bundle again. He took a deep breath, then another, calming himself as the shock fell from him in tumbling veils.

The woman who had led to the momentary relapse had long since passed but, although embarrassed by his edginess, he still looked back fearfully over his shoulder.

*   *   *

Turning right he wandered down a side path that deteriorated into a muddy track before snaking off through a wood of dead elms. Looking down he saw the serrated grasses cutting at his ankles as the weeds and brambles (as if knowing what he had in mind) fought to slow his progress. He crouched down when close-by in the undergrowth, something moved. Seemingly totally oblivious to his presence (and the incessant buzzing of flies) a small Jack Russell terrier was snuffling in the underbrush, its head jerking around as if an unseen puppet master was pulling it on strings.

He heard a voice.

A short way off a young woman with long luxuriant dark hair strode through the brambles, a dog's lead hanging limply from her left hand as she trailed words behind her.

He felt possessed by the things he craved: silence and blackness and darkness. His bitterness was his defence against the world as he was determined never to be the whipping-boy again.

He hunched further down, mentally whispering to himself, preparing...

He felt dead inside as he had sold his soul one sin at a time until only a dark void now remained.

His eyes narrowed to slits as he watched the unfurling scene... then abruptly his eyes snapped open as he plunged the knife deep within the back of her neck. Small droplets of blood were sent flying through the air as she opened her mouth to scream in shock and pain, but no sound would come, just a deep gurgling within her throat as blood filled her mouth and cold deep panic filled her gut. She stumbled forward, blinded by tears, feeling nothing but searing pain. She glanced fearfully back over her shoulder to find no one there, just the sound of chilling footsteps clicking over broken twigs, creeping towards her, closing in on her.

Blood dripped from her chin as the final wheezing gasps of breath bubbled through the blood in her throat. As she found herself stumbling forward, slipping on something slimy in the brambles, her mind shrieked at the vision of her garroted pet. That was the last thing she saw as, immobilized by shock, the cold steel blade again rushed towards her gaping throat...

CHAPTER 4

THE SEARCH

As Detective Sergeant Armstrong approached the crime scene he saw that the area was already in the process of being meticulously photographed and surveyed. The crime scene examiners, who were all attired in their familiar white jumpsuits and latex gloves were now crouched down inside the perimeter of the barrier tape, which was yellow in colour and issued the seemingly not too veiled threat of 'Police Line: Do not cross'.

The air was moist and mild and erected search lights were casting greenish-white beams, shafts of foggy light across the long grass.

He saw that Detective Inspector Ross was already present and had apparently assumed control, whilst in front of him uniformed police officers were trying to usher the assembled crowd still further back behind the police line. As it had been impossible to keep the police activity quiet, media trucks and local residents had descended upon the area like a plague of locusts. The general public were there, devouring the unfurling events with glee, because they were witnessing the ultimate in reality television. The press were there because their livelihoods at stake.

Sucking in his breath, he inwardly despaired at the society the human race had now created, gene pools that made puddles appear deep.

He glanced down at his wristwatch and realized that as it was now approaching seven o'clock in the evening, they had less than an hour of daylight left. He knew that searching the crime scene in the half-light would prove to be a logistical nightmare, so fancied that he would be recalled at first light tomorrow to continue with the search.

He flashed his identity badge as he reached the uniformed police officers standing guard of the cordoned off perimeter and ducked below the crime scene ribbon to enter the open space.

Wind swept the long grass whilst the darkening sky above was swollen with a waiting deluge, so Mother Nature was obviously in a cleansing mood.

In the shadowed gloom, Detective Inspector Ross stood central, arms folded across his chest, barking out orders to anyone that fell within earshot. He was hoping to instil a sense of urgency to the operation, though fully aware that he could not touch anything until it had been meticulously studied, photographed and logged. He noted that the earlier rain and overcast sky appeared to be hindering the crime scene officer's work.

He acknowledged Detective Sergeant Armstrong's arrival with a nod of the head.

"Evening Governor, have we got anything?"

Instead of answering immediately, Detective Inspector Ross shifted uneasily from foot to foot before replying.

"Not yet. We don't even have a name for her as there was no identification on the body and so far no handbag or purse has been found. Could possibly be a robbery that went wrong. The only jewellery she had on was a wedding band but, unfortunately for us, there is no engraving on it."

"Who called it in?"

"A local woman, who was out walking her dog in the open space. She seemed on the level, but had to be whisked off to hospital suffering from shock, so details are still quite patchy at this stage. Detective Sergeant Sandra Ryder is still with her and will ring us as soon as there is any news regarding her being declared fit enough to be interviewed."

Their eyes momentarily locked before they looked across at the pools of dried blood that had stained the grass. Samples of the bloodstains had already been picked up on gauze pads by the evidence recovery personnel and logged, prior to being taken to the laboratory for analysis.

As Detective Inspector Ross once again glanced at the slain bodies of the woman and her dog he could not help but feel an enormous wave of tenderness and pity wash over him.

Greeted by the curiously melancholy sight he felt a shiver shoot down his spine and greasy fingers of nausea seize his guts. Around the edges of his eyes crow's feet gathered, emphasizing his bleak, dry anger.

As far as he could tell the woman had stab wounds to the neck and back and although her eyes were still open she was quite clearly dead. Blood stains had soaked into her cascading brunette hair (so that it now hung down in rats tails) and her clothing, which appeared to consist of faded blue jeans and a black woollen jumper. The sight of her halted and held his breath, though it vibrated in his windpipe and threatened to make him gag. He momentarily closed his eyes and strove to suppress the welling of anxiety within him. He found a tear creeping down his cheek and was grateful that it seemingly went unnoticed by the other officers who were stood nearby. Realizing the need to stay in control he quickly brushed it away with the back of his hand and sucked in a choked breath. He gulped to ease his throat which had gone unexpectedly dry. The last year had filled his heart with a terrible despondency and grief, which was now beginning to brim with anger. He adjusted his position and checked his wristwatch, buying time in which to regain his sense of composure.

Detective Sergeant Armstrong, although no canine expert recognized the breed of dog immediately due to its docked tail and black saddle on coarse white fur. His eyes had widened in alarm, as at first he was disbelieving as to what he was viewing. He could not speak and just stood shaking his head. Momentarily overcome by immense sorrow and pity, he felt as powerless as a ghost. For some reason the vision of the garroted pet had choked him just as much as the woman's fate. Perhaps it was true what they said about the English and their love of animals after all…

After a short and somewhat awkward pause Detective Inspector Ross brought him up to date on the state of play. The photographer and photographic log recorder had captured the site and the evidence recovery personnel had begun the task of collecting and packaging evidence samples. The medical examiner had assessed the bodies and was currently dictating a preliminary report into his trusted Dictaphone.

Detective Sergeant Armstrong could not help but note the quiver of frustration and desperation in Detective Inspector Ross's voice. Obviously the search was not going too well and he suspected that it would now be widened. The search was predominantly looking for a discarded knife or gloves, but any trace evidence would obviously be a welcome find.

The hunt for the serial killer had drained them both, mentally and physically, draining them of colour and energy, and it showed.

Lost in their own thoughts, their eyes locked for a brief moment before returning to the slain bodies, the shock of what they were seeing, again seemingly paralyzing them and freezing the moment.

Off in the distance the media hysteria was now in full flow, as voices loud and resonant projected towards them. The press and media insults, on the lines of how ineffectual they were, had accompanied them both to the site, but they now seemed to be getting a second wind. Detective Inspector Ross frowned as he looked across at Detective Sergeant Armstrong, as the officers could almost taste the hostility that lay in wait there but could not risk any unwise words to the heckling reporters landing either of them in trouble. Shaking their heads in disbelief, defensive anger rose within them, the crowd's insistence only fuelling the heat of their temper. Fortunately they were both fully accustomed to hiding those feelings and keeping their cool under such intense provocation. But although they remained silent, they subconsciously showed their displeasure by tightening their lips and stiffening their shoulders, their breath growing stale in their lungs as they lapsed into silence.

Under the declining sun, powerful lamps had been brought to the scene as it had needed to be meticulously searched and photographed. As usual the officers were looking for tyre prints, footprints and any discarded weapons or clothing. Detective Inspector Ross had been hoping that the search would yield a harvest of information, but so far the designated search had turned up nothing of note and he desperately needed something to go on, in order to construct a workable case.

The medical examiner's team had now arrived, so the bodies encased in wrapping sheets and body bags were removed to the morgue with minimal fuss.

Detective Inspector Ross, who had previously been taking extensive notes, looked down at the pen and writing pad clutched tightly in his hands, now aware that his fingers had turned white. He closed his pad before slipping it back inside his jacket pocket with the pen. He lifted his cuff and looked down nervously at his wristwatch, which seemed to be ticking as loudly as a grandfather clock, perhaps sensing that time was working against him.

It had been a typical English summer's day, so the afternoon's rain had made the ground sodden, making searching for clues amongst the wind churned long grass, discarded litter and loose broken twigs a somewhat thankless task. Police officers and crime scene investigators armed with torches, police tape and evidence bags were crouched down, side by side, on their hands and knees, combing designated areas, alert for discarded evidence, ideally the murder weapon.

With the light now fading rapidly the search would soon need to be stood down until they could resume at first light the next day. This was not ideal as public areas were notoriously difficult, if not impossible, to keep secure until they had been thoroughly processed. The potential for contamination still existed but Detective Inspector Ross just hoped that the barrier tape, which would remain in the interim as well as a patrol car with minimal personnel, would be enough to keep any ghoulish souvenir hunters at bay until the investigation was complete. Hopefully mementos of the occasion would not be appearing on the eBay website at any time soon.

He turned his attention to the somber sky. The rain had just begun to fall once more, dampening what had already proved to be a fruitless enquiry. With the thin drizzle, the air now felt fresh and damp against his skin. The flashing lights of the police cars made shadows spring across the ground, capturing water drops glistening on the blades of grass that danced rhythmically in the evening breeze. In the distance cars dragged their headlight beams over the sodden ground as engines rumbled to life.

Car tyre ruts were now deeply etched into the ground and rain beaded on their surface as it started to fall harder. The ground remained subtly lit but was still heavily layered with sheltering shadows. The hard darkness only penetrated by the tears of the Gods that were currently being shed as if mourning their plight.

Detective Inspector Ross had been hoping the rain would disperse some of the assembled throng, but at present they seemed static and grim-faced.

He realized that there were certain duties and responsibilities, which were necessary in any major investigation but deep inside he was dreading having to make an impromptu press statement, as the search had so far yielded nothing of note. He knew that he must not lose his courage.

Shadowed in the gloom between the shrubs he stood forlornly, feeling angry and frustrated at the evening's events, his mind churning with conflicting currents.

The events had carved his face, painting a dull stream of desperation in his eyes and sculpting his features into that of a tormented man.

With a hint of testiness in his voice he stood the crime scene personnel down and watched as they loaded the evidence samples taken into their vehicles and departed, cutting a swath through the gathered lynch mop, who still seemed determined to play a part in the unfolding drama.

With a shake of his head, he turned away from Detective Sergeant Armstrong and gazed over at the assembled spectators.

The thin drizzle had now become driving rain, so that his shirt now stuck to his expanding waistline, which was a more than vivid testimony to his lifestyle of fast food and real ale. Unexpectedly the crowd remained, stood in deepening puddles, as unlike him most had the foresight to bring umbrellas or appropriate clothing with them. He looked across at the rows of hooded men and umbrella covered women, wondering how sad their lives must be if this was their idea of family entertainment.

One particularly thuggish looking individual with a shaven head and face like a pit bull terrier held a copy of the Daily Star over his bald pate, obviously too stupid to realize that the rivulets of wet print, from a variety of third rate topless models, were now cascading down his face, staining his features before dripping onto his white sweatshirt, thus marking that too.

With the heavy rain Detective Inspector Ross's own, once luxuriant grey hair, now sat plastered upon his scalp like a squashed rodent.

With the rapidly diminishing light he felt shrouded in disgruntled misery.

It was at that point that a ghostly laugh emanated from the assembled crowd, which seemed wholly inappropriate considering the tragic events that had just befallen the area.

Detective Inspector Ross's face contorted into a grimace of fury and disgust, his grief momentarily gone but only to be replaced by smouldering anger. Rage filled him with a trembling heat as resentment poured in. He locked the crowd with a baleful stare as rage shook his voice. He turned and roared to the uniformed officers nearest to him, struggling to regain control as his body shook with explosive anger, their curiosity finally wearing on his nerves.

"Get these bloody vultures away from my crime scene immediately."

As the officers went about their task, the howls and jeers from the assembled mob intensified as if locked in a state of mutual resentment, their expressions baleful.

Detective Sergeant Armstrong had remained silent through most of this but now assisted the uniformed officers in dispersing the crowd. Fortunately the combination of the elements, brute force and coercion was now starting to make an impact as slowly but surely the human cockroaches scuttled away.

The heavy driving rain was now partially obscuring the figures as they departed, so as Detective Inspector Ross watched, his eyes pinched at the corners straining to see, it seemed as though he was viewing them in some grainy B-movie.

Though pleased to see them depart, his face had still taken on a look of exasperation as he acknowledged his failure to maintain his control. He reflected, deep in thought, retreating into his own thoughts and feeling more than a little uncomfortable with them.

His mobile phone, as if sensing his downward mood, suddenly chirped to life. Sliding his hand into his jacket pocket, he removed it before flicking it open to speak.

"Hello, Detective Inspector Ross."

The familiar voice of Detective Chief Inspector Andy Burns greeted him, so obviously someone had managed to prize him away from the golf clubhouse.

He demanded a full account of the events but as the reception kept cutting in and out, he was forced to agree on a briefing first thing the next morning.

Finishing the conversation, Detective Inspector Ross flipped the phone shut before replacing it back into his pocket. As he did so Detective Sergeant Armstrong came alongside him.

"Was that the Detective Chief Inspector?"

"Yeah, wants a briefing first thing tomorrow. He is probably planning on a press call. Let's get packed up here and we can have a swift half. After today I need a drink. You follow me."

Huddled against the downpour, heads bowed, they walked quickly to their respective cars, before tugging at the boot releases to deposit their torches and police tape. Detective Inspector Ross turned to the remaining officers to leave them their final few instructions. A relief crew would be summoned but until then they would need to protect the crime scene.

The officers acknowledged his instructions, so on opening the driver's door he fell into the driver's seat. After a brief hesitation he gripped the steering wheel and pressed himself further back into the seat. As he listened to the rain whipping against the windscreen and drumming upon the roof, he sat slumped behind the wheel. He was glad to finally get the weight off of his feet.

He had never before felt so alone in a crowd.

He momentarily closed his eyes and slumped against the driver's side door, supporting his weight on his right side, as a mixture of perspiration and droplets of rain fell from his beaded brow.

The pine scented air freshener that was adhered to the dashboard did nothing to mask the smell of stale cigarette smoke and so the air inside the car held memories of his own addiction, one that he was still battling somewhat unsuccessfully.

Looking into the rear view mirror he noted that his eyes, full of unnerving pensiveness, looked weary and dejected and his lined face heavy with regret. A nagging thought hovered below the surface of his mind but he was too fatigued for it to come to the fore.

Disrupting his train of thought, he acknowledged his failure. Although he was born into a catholic family he had never had the inclination to confess to a guy in a frock, so had always kept his burden and guilt very much within, much to the detriment of his health…

He wished that he could rein in his emotions, back onto safer ground.

He knew that he did not deserve to be in such torment, but was unsure as to how he might find the inner peace he so desperately sought. Bitterness and happiness seemed to be dealt by the hands of fate, rather than by his own decisions. He seemed powerless to change the current situation. He was overcome by a sense of futility and weariness.

To escape this moment of distraction and the crouching darkness, Ross slipped the key into the ignition. The engine spluttered into life before purring its response. The steering wheel vibrated slightly as the windscreen wipers stutteringly chased droplets of the silvery rain towards the edges of the windshield.

Detective Inspector Ross revved the engine before lurching out, inching forward through the water that lay in heavy puddles on the ground, dragging the car's headlights through the glittering rain and over the sodden ground. As the fall of rain hissed and roared and with the decline into night, other cars were departing at the same time but he saw Detective Sergeant Armstrong fall in smoothly behind him.

As he checked back in his rear view mirror he saw the lone police car stood lit amongst the glow of the tail lights, guarding the scene as if it were a silent monument to those who had fallen. Its swirling light ceaselessly restless making tangled distorted shadows that looked like a pack of dogs chasing their tails. The area felt haunted, its stillness full of eerie and disturbing expectation.

As he wiped his rain-splattered face on his sleeve and pushed back the darkened silver hair that the rain had plastered to his skull, he sensed that it was going to be a very long night…

CHAPTER 5

LONDON TOWN

Karl Connor had always liked the capital at dawn, as daybreak offered promise of a fresh beginning and because it was too early for there to be anyone else around.

He welcomed the solitude after what had been a long and often troublesome journey to reach this point in his life. There were no prying eyes or inquisitive mouths. In his world silence was indeed golden.

As he sat perched upon the white birch window seat a profound peace settled on his soul. Lost deep within his own thoughts, he ignored the unmade bed and lolling duvet that pleaded for his return and instead gazed out at the sky, watching for several hours as it changed colour from warm grey to pastel blue. The pale blue sky was later decorated with wind-torn strips of cloud.

His recent mood had been up and down like a fiddler's elbow, but at present he felt relaxed and calm, at ease with himself and tranquil.

Taking a deep breath he finally arose and striding across the room he flicked on the stereo, inviting the American twang of John Cougar Mellancamp to fill the room.

He realized that the memory of his victims had now become hazy and dreamlike. He needed fuel for his fantasy life; it was time to kill again.

He could feel his penis stiffen in his pants at the thought of his emotional baggage being lightened by vengeful fury, eager to taste the bitter fruits that life had to offer.

Detection held no fear for him, as he would end it himself when the time was right. He had always known that you were born alone into this life and that any relationships were just a distractive illusion on the pathway to death.

He held no belief in his immortal soul as his mortal one had already given him too much tumult, hence the end held no fear for him.

He found himself sweating from a combination of the heat and the thrill of his impending mission, eager to once again experience the delight of life being drained away.

He ran his hand absently through his fair hair as he headed towards the bathroom, eager to bathe and dress. He sank down into the bubble bath and languished in its warmth as it lapped over his submerged body, massaging his muscles. After a few minutes he scrubbed himself before climbing out feeling refreshed and invigorated. As he towelled himself dry, the final trickle of bubbling water was sucked relentlessly into the unplugged whirlpool, before it let out a satisfied belch. He ran a comb through his hair and cleaned his teeth, before wrapping a towel around his waist like a skirt and trailing wet footprints behind him all the way to the bedroom.

When he finally reappeared in the living room he was attired in a freshly starched white cotton shirt and a smart charcoal suit. Although, as usual, he had no employment to go to, he felt that one should always make the most of one's self and put one's best foot forward...

He stood in front of the mirror for a few moments, enjoying the vision that greeted him.

*   *   *

Closing the front door behind him, he walked briskly up the short path to the front gate. He stopped after a couple of steps and surveyed the scene.

His large Victorian house with leafy, peaceful private garden was typical for the area and afforded him a warm glow of achievement.

He took in a deep breath, his lungs filling with the sun-kissed air.

The weather forecast had been positive and no more rain had been predicted for a good few days.

Making the most of his freedom he eased himself into his silver grey metallic BMW M3 convertible, slipping comfortably behind the wheel as he admired the gleaming paintwork and nappa leather seats.

Reaching over to his left, he flipped open the glove compartment that held his compact disks, sunglasses, a bottle of still mineral water, leather gloves, a couple of pens, a notebook and a London A-Z. Squinting against the sunlight he reached inside and grabbed his sunglasses and Jon Bon Jovi's: 'Blaze of Glory' compact disc, the latter of which he removed from its case and eased gently into the stereo system. He then drew the sunglasses down over his eyes and checked himself in the mirror, feeling suitably impressed with what he saw. With the glaring sunlight, his honey blond hair glinted with reflective shine, giving him an almost Scandinavian look.

He then reached across for the seatbelt that hung rigid like a charmed cobra and pulled it tightly across his chest before clicking it into position.

He turned the key in the ignition and let the engine quietly purr to life before pulling out into the road. He flicked on the radio, hoping to catch any traffic bulletins from the flying eye, but instead was greeted with the nasal tones of Dido, an artist who in his opinion had somehow managed to turn bland elevator music into a multi million pound art form, which was quite some achievement...mind you Phil Collins had done the same previously. Perhaps it was a sign of the times, that with the right marketing strategy, you could sell ice to Eskimos...

Giving up on the idea of listening to the radio station, he pressed the button to open the driver's window and sparked the compact disc player to life.

Jon Bon Jovi began to sing his own unique version of stadium rock, thankfully drowning out voices raised in an argument from the car that currently sat alongside him. Glancing over at their car, Karl could not help but to notice that its red paintwork was heavily dappled with white deposits, as if it had been recently bombarded by the avian equivalent of Jeremy Beadle.

Karl noticed that both the teenage occupants were attired in Burberry baseball caps and cheap gold jewellery so chunky that it looked as though they had just mugged Mr. T, so obviously neither taste nor decorum were very high on their list of requisites.

Thankfully the traffic lights soon changed and they sped off, leaving black burning rubber on the road as they did so, their voices thankfully trailing away.

Gliding through the busy streets, Karl eyed the pavements that were already bustling with shoppers and office workers, the latter of which were stood like lepers outside their work premises, huddled together, feverishly chain-smoking the cancer sticks that were gripped firmly between their yellowing nicotine stained fingers. The thought of their weak wills could not help but bring a self-satisfied smirk to his face.

His eyes momentarily swam out of focus as his memory pulled up visions from the past...

Flooded with anticipation, the knowledge that he was moving invisibly through a world of potential victims oblivious to him elevated his mood still further.

As he continued with his planned route through Notting Hill Gate, he could not fail to notice the stench from the burger, kebab and Asian take-away houses that greased the air. It led him to ponder as to why it was no longer possible to purchase English cuisine. It seemed odd, as it was the host country.

Whatever happened to the old greasy spoon cafes and the pie and mash shops that used to be seen as outlets for staple diets in days gone by? Surely it could not be a result of people's attempts at healthy eating as he failed to see how mechanically recovered meat in a toasted sesame seed bun, Southern fried rodent or sweet and sour feline could be classed in any way, shape or form as any step up the culinary ladder. He smiled thinly as he found modern life a conundrum that often left him in a perpetual state of bewilderment.

He had now become part of the usual London traffic standstill, so he sat absorbing the unfolding scene as the music filtered through the air around him.

He watched as market stall vendors, clad in green cotton aprons, tried to get frazzled looking passersby to purchase some of their array of fresh fruit and vegetables that were stacked on their well stocked wooden barrows.

Alongside them, hot dog and beef burger venders unsuccessfully tried to tempt the milling general public with their salmonella and E. coli ridden offerings. As the fried onions sizzled on the hot plates next to sausages, burgers and an army of flies, the assorted passersby, unsurprisingly, looked less than keen to try their own particular version of culinary Russian roulette.

Up ahead he could hear hammering and drilling resonating, that assaulted his senses and as he neared the infernal din, he closed his window to mask the cacophony of noise and to avoid the billowing clouds of pale dust that had started to drift up in front of him. He coughed to clear his throat, before he flicked up the stereo a notch or two, so that Jon Bon Jovi who had previously tried to convince everyone that he was a cowboy, was now positively screaming his pretensions.

As Karl passed the building site he glanced out of the driver's side window at the hairy-arsed builders that were clinging to scaffolding as if they were apes in a zoo.

It caused the infinite monkey theorem to flick through his mind and he pondered how long it would take them to erect such a building to the same standard. Would give them something to do after their literary careers have peaked...

A car horn blared behind him as the traffic light had changed to green. Moving off slowly he found that the traffic was still bumper-to-bumper and there appeared to be no vacant parking spaces. He could sense his patience wearing thin as it was a hot, listless summer's day, with no wind at play, and not the ideal weather to be stuck inside a tin can, however top of the range it may be.

He felt growing apprehension at the realization that he may have to abort his intended mission. Karl's heart sank a little. He knew that he needed to make another kill as, try as he might, he could not hold the previous memories in all their initial vividness. Besides, he enjoyed the attention and media coverage that his actions were attracting and so was loath to cancel today's jaunt, he was determined but not recklessly so. He did not want to lose momentum with the police and the media, as there would always be other news stories, always someone out there trying to steal his thunder.

He was inclined to believe that there would be more chance of him understanding the new off-side rule in football than with the police ever catching up with him. He suspected that he would be alright as long as he did not allow paranoia to kick in. He could feel it simmering away under all his thoughts and still when he wasn't thinking. His mind seemed like a vacuum, sponging up stimuli without subtext and anxiety, drawing everything to it like a magnet in his head, every little problem amplified and contorted.

However this game ended he knew that he would go down in history and would be spoken about for a great many years to come. It was a shame that he may not be able to enjoy it but he knew if caught that he could never spend the rest of his natural life in jail. He was determined to ensure that he would never be incarcerated again…

CHAPTER 6

POST MORTEM

The female body had initially been tagged and photographed, both clothed and unclothed. It was then x-rayed, weighed and measured, with identifying marks recorded. Trace evidence, hair and fibres, were collected off the body, and the nails clipped, before being sent with the clothes for analysis. Once the body was clean, it was laid out face up on a steel table with a stabilizing block placed under her head, for the detailed examination to begin in earnest.

It was Detective Inspector Ross who had attended the post-mortem, and for a man of such vast police experience he found himself surprisingly moved by the sight of the autopsy.

He watched it with burning anger welling up inside him, a familiar taste of guilt, whilst a personal vow to catch the murderer smoldered in his mind. A quiver passed through him and he just hoped that he was not exposing himself to fresh anguish.

He sucked in a bitter breath, as he looked on, his expression irritable.

As the death was not natural, the medical examiner recorded the circumstances surrounding the death, along with all the available information at his disposal about the deceased person. He then recorded the results of the external examination and listed all the physical characteristics, including weight and height.

With the local serial murders he'd had many strangulation cases of late, but this clearly was not to be one of them…

As he narrated to the voice recorder his voice was flat, studiedly emotionless, but almost a whisper. He stated that he was going to make a Y-incision, taking care to avoid the existing knife wounds, although after he had finished it, Detective Inspector Ross thought it looked more like a U with a tail.

He definitely would not have fancied him performing a circumcision…

Samples were taken of fluid in the organs and the stomach and intestines were opened to examine the contents. The medical examiner continued with the examination before confirming the cause and approximate time of death.

Once the examination was over and all the details recorded, the medical examiner, who was a small man, portly and jovial, signed the official form and began stripping off his latex gloves as Detective Inspector Ross spoke.

"So, what's the conclusion?"

"Nothing you do not already know I suspect. There were two knife wounds – one stab wound to the back of the neck, just above the shoulder blades, which would have been non fatal and the second was a cutting motion to the throat, from which she bled to death. No other wounds, no defence cuts, so either she knew her attacker or was taken by complete surprise…or both."

Detective Inspector Ross sucked in a weary breath as he mulled over the information.

"How long would it have taken for her to die?"

"Mercifully for her, death would have been almost instantaneous."

As the pathologist answered, his breath, which peppermints had not much disguised, was a stale mixture of tobacco and garlic, and was bad enough to make Detective Inspector Ross take an involuntary step back.

"I take it we now have a positive identification?"

"Yes, her name is Lisa Browne. Her husband reported her missing and has since identified the body. I had to give her a 'quickie makeover' for his benefit, but it is definitely her though."

Remembering certain misidentifications in the past Detective Inspector Ross thought it best to hammer the point home.

"So there can be no doubt?"

"No, I have confirmed the identification through her dental records."

Detective Inspector Ross grumbled an acceptance, before continuing.

"Estimated time of death?"

"It was probably somewhere between 7am and midday. She had traces of caffeine and bread in her stomach contents, so I am assuming that was her breakfast of toast and coffee."

"What about the murder weapon?"

"It was almost certainly a long bladed hunting knife."

With the coronial investigation completed and the manner of death now officially confirmed Detective Inspector Ross thanked the pathologist and bid him farewell, his mind was already racing ahead of him. The recent serial killer cases had troubled his days and haunted his nights. He would just have to pray that the evidence that was taken away to the forensic laboratory, as well as the new dog walker murder evidence, heralded some much needed clues. With every passing day he could feel the noose of dismissal tightening around his neck.

As he exited the building and entered the car park, he looked across at a group of pigeons that were nodding to crumbs on the tarmac, just for that moment wishing that he could swap places with them, as they appeared so carefree, answerable to no one. Their whole lives revolving around pecking at discarded food before searching out freshly cleaned laundry and vehicles on which to deposit their waste, as if they were winged jesters.

He shoved his hands into the pockets of his trousers as he gazed dolefully down at his shoes. Turning inward he held the pain close.

When he looked up, he noticed that the sky had clouded over, the sudden gloom mirroring his currently pessimistic thoughts.

Suddenly he felt inexorably alone with his thoughts, whilst the knowledge that his failure to catch the serial killer had led to unnecessary murders tore at his mind. Now he had this new murder to contend with.

It had so far been a long journey of countless small steps and he felt wasted.

Until he was fully rested, he knew that he could no longer trust his senses or his hunches. He felt the need to go home, desperate for some sleep and a chance to de-stress, but he knew that as he was heavily swamped with paperwork, his office would be the only place that he would be going. The cases continued to hold him in their vice like grip as a cold shiver prickled at his skin. He knew that initially he had concentrated on the wrong man, to the detriment of the enquiry, so it would be up to him to make amends. His eyes twitched as he struggled to banish the memory. Enlightenment did not rise within him as he felt weary and exhausted, battered by the trauma of the day. He was a runaway train of emotions and he knew that he needed to regain control of himself and the case.

After all this was over he felt that he would sleep for a year…

CHAPTER 7

ALMOST INESCAPABLE

Karl shuffled his shirt sleeve up and looked down at his watch. It had just gone a half past three.

He glanced over out of his living room window, watching as a traffic warden sauntered by. Just a brief moment later and heading in the same direction a frazzled looking gentleman went hurrying by, seemingly in pursuit of the warden. Karl watched the ensuing argument as bystanders always do when those kind of confrontations (between over-zealous traffic wardens and hapless motorists) occur, mentally egging on the driver to land a right hook on them.

Strangely on this occasion the visibly relieved and grateful motorist was allowed to proceed on his way seemingly without a parking ticket being issued.

Wonders would never cease…

Karl could only assume that either the traffic warden had already made a note of the illegally parked vehicle's registration number prior to the owner's arrival on the scene and would write up the parking ticket long after the event or else he did not receive a bonus for every ticket that was issued.

With the temporary moment of excitement seemingly passed Karl came away from the window and wandered through into the kitchen to prepare himself a pot of tea.

Once the kettle had boiled and switched itself off with a resounding click he filled the teapot with the scalding liquid, soaking the two teabags that already lay in wait at the bottom of the vessel.

He left the tea to brew for a short while and entered the living room to switch on the television set. The screen sparked an image to life and a quiz show hostess appeared, cackling like some deranged crone.

The quiz show 'Countdown' must have changed its time slot as he had always managed to avoid it since his first unscheduled and never to be forgotten viewing.

If television programmes could be described as colours then this one would surely be beige.

Karl was shocked to see that it was now sponsored by Specsavers opticians when surely Mogadon would have been a far more appropriate backer?!

Strangely the programme had acquired a new host since his last unfortunate viewing and now Des Lynam (or 'the-thinking-woman-of-a-certain-age's crumpet' as he was now better known) appeared to have taken over the show's reins. He looked as bored as Karl felt and seemed totally disinterested and not a little embarrassed to be on the programme – a feeling that obviously Karl could well relate to. With its almost coma inducing pacing, it would have run a close second to an arthritic tortoise.

Juggling with the endless burden of having witless presenters and staid format, Karl had never quite understood the seemingly wide and long running appeal of that particular programme.

Karl was about to reach for the remote control to switch over channels when the quiz show hostess appeared again, a vision that momentarily shocked him. He had seen her plugging and advocating many diets and de-tox regimes over the recent years, yet there she stood with a figure more easily described as 'chunky' than 'slinky'. Not that he felt there was anything amiss with women having a fuller figure of course but he did not see how such people could then endorse such dietary products without having at least a pang of guilty conscience over their double standards, especially when she had obviously been 'specially lit' and 'air-brushed' to within an inch of her life during the campaigns...

Karl let the thought drift and wondered as to why he was getting so hot under the collar over such trivial matters.

He really did need to start getting out more...

He finally managed to switch the television channel over before padding back into the kitchen to pour out the tea (before it had become too stewed in the pot).

He emptied a couple of heaped teaspoonfuls of granulated sugar into the waiting china cup, before adding the boiling tea and finishing up with a generous splash of cold semi-skimmed milk. He gave the tan-coloured liquid a quick stir so that the sugar was fully dissolved before casting the teaspoon aside into the empty sink basin.

Picking up the cup and saucer he re-entered the living room in time to catch the 3:35pm news bulletin which was just about to begin on Channel Five.

The female newsreader had put on the expression that all news presenters and front-bench politicians were trained to assume when conveying news items that were either deemed grim or depressing...or both.

The report on this occasion related to the case of the female dog walker who had been brutally murdered in the local area several days earlier. The lady in question had now been formally identified as a Mrs. Lisa Browne of Uxbridge Street, W8.

The newsreader vanished from view as the picture switched to the crime scene. The area was still swarming with police, police dogs and vehicles and the entire location appeared to positively swimming in a deluge of yellow and black crime scene tape.

A small crowd of onlookers had gathered, bunched in small clusters beyond the tape, no doubt seeking to get their faces in front of the assorted television cameras in order to be able to relive their brief and fleeting moment of infamy via their video recorders for many years to come.

To think that would be the heights of their achievement made Karl feel ashamed and embarrassed for the loathsome insects.

As Karl watched the unfurling scene and the live report that was now being aired he surprisingly felt somewhat detached but then a photograph of Lisa Browne was flashed up upon the screen. The broadcast then cut back to the television studio where Lisa Browne's distraught family and a uniformed police officer began appealing for witnesses and even the murderer to come forward.

At that point he felt a slight pang of conscience and terminated the programme, the screen growing as black as his soul.

Why had he not had a family as obviously caring as that when he was a child…?

Why had no one ever cared about him…?

His mind tumbled back in time as if relishing the retelling of the ugly details, the decline into enveloping darkness.

Such things, no matter how hard he tried, seemed almost inescapable.

When Karl eventually snapped to, he noted that the sky outside had clouded over readying no doubt to spill another lashing of summer rain on the increasingly frazzled English public. Quite why (with global warming seemingly melting the polar icecaps and the Earth apparently turning into a giant furnace) did the British summer still tend to consist of a few rain-free days each year, he mused wistfully.

It was a conundrum that left both him and he assumed most of the country perplexed.

He took a sip of tea before carefully replacing his cup and saucer onto the coffee table.

As he cast his gaze out through the partially opened window he saw that it had now begun to rain – a thin drizzle but enough to dampen his already sagging spirits still further.

He felt the pang of hunger overtake him but he was in no real mood to prepare an elaborate meal.

Getting up from the soft leather settee he meandered through to the kitchen area to prepare himself a couple of toasted cheese and tomato sandwiches.

Karl ate the first sandwich and then the second in rapid succession. As he savoured the hot melted butter mingling with the melted cheese he could sense his previously forlorn mood raising slightly.

Sometimes the simple pleasures in life were among the ones that felt the best.

Unfortunately tasty food nearly always tended to be high in fat content so he knew that he would have to burn off the extra calories later and not be spending what remained of the day reliving the decay that his childhood had provided (the revenge, the anger and the misery of rejection) or sat glued to the television set like some dull couch potato.

There had to be more to life than that – there just had to be...

An hour later

The pavement underfoot was, of course, still slightly damp from the earlier deluge but thankfully the sun had momentarily decided to pop its reluctant head through the assembled clouds that were waiting anxiously in the wings.

Karl walked down the high street in the direction of Notting Hill Gate tube station. As he did so he could not help but to note that the grass verges had been recently trimmed and, despite the obligatory assorted items of discarded litter, looked a brilliant fresh green and almost seemed to be glowing under the yellow clouded sunset.

As he rounded the corner a newsagent's display board (situated on the opposite side of the road) caught his eye. He could only read part of the main headline and not any other smaller print underneath, so curiosity impelled him to cross over the carriageway, picking his way gingerly through the assorted vehicles that were momentarily sat frozen at the traffic lights that shone a blazing red.

The newsagent was still open so he entered to purchase a copy of the late edition of the London Evening Standard.

As Karl exited the shop premises he instinctively began to flick through the pages, eager to soak up the glory that the printed words would hopefully offer him. As he read the article his assurance increased. The investigating police force apparently had no possible suspect although the obligatory line 'following a number of lines of enquiry' had appeared. This did not worry him unduly as it seemingly accompanied every press and media release that the police had ever made. He supposed that it sounded more reassuring to the general British public than the truth, 'Sorry folks, we have not got a clue who the killer is but we are chuffed with the amount of overtime we are receiving on this enquiry.'

At present he was only interested in the news items that related directly to him so once he had devoured the latest press release he screwed up the publication and deposited it into the first litter bin that he came to.

As Karl approached the dismally grey and uninviting subway entrance to Notting Hill Gate underground tube station he was stopped in his tracks by a crowd of people stood in front of a human barricade of uniformed London Transport staff.

Amid the many heated discussions that were currently taking place Karl managed to establish that the London underground network had temporarily been suspended due to a terrorist alert and as a result the tube station was closed until further notice.

Karl obviously realized that the London commuters would now all be packing themselves onto buses so that they resembled sardines in a tin or else attempting to hail taxi cabs whose drivers would have been doubling their usual prices within seconds of the transport news being broadcast over their respective radios.

Karl decided that travelling by road would prove to be a nightmare so he decided to forgo his original intention of heading into central London for a meal in Chinatown before catching a late night film at one of the numerous cinemas within the Leicester Square area and instead turned and made his way back to the Pembridge Road, heading towards a public house called 'Mook', which he had recalled passing on the way to the tube station.

Although, as a rule, he was not a great advocate of public houses he had now decided to give it a shot.

He began to walk in the direction from which he had just come and as he walked he edged passed little shops and cafes, resisting their silent but visually alluring attempts to entice him in.

A fine, almost smoky, rain had just begun to fall so Karl quickened his pace. Minutes later he had arrived at his renewed destination.

Although it was still relatively early in the evening the 'Mook' bar was already buzzing with clientele, no doubt as a result of the same transport restrictions that had so abruptly curtailed his own departure from the surrounding district. The atmosphere inside the establishment was homely and cool but without being pretentious.

When the bartender took his order Karl was doubly shocked, firstly that the barman was not Australian (he had not realized that public houses in London still employed non-Antipodean staff) and secondly that the drinks were reasonably priced (and not being sold at the heavily marked-up tourist rate that seemed to have blighted most of London's hostelries.

As Karl found himself a vacant seat, far away from the main throng of activity, he viewed the unfolding scenes with interest. He had always loved to study human interaction, observing the character traits and, more importantly, their flaws.

They would prove to be no more than pawns in his game…

As he scanned the establishment's interior he saw that it had a lot of style; a warmly lit bar which no doubt as well as the good music created a fun atmosphere and a good vibe for all concerned – the staff as well as patrons.

Usually he would wish to be free of chart music, fruit machines and young vacuous people but tonight he did not care. He relished the temporary distraction from his usual routines and from the ghosts that were never too far from his consciousness, attempting to punish him for the violence, the cruelty and the simple unkindness that had tainted his very soul. For a brief time he would feel cleansed and liberated.

As he took a healthy gulp of his rich red wine he wondered where, how and with whom the night would end…

CHAPTER 8

THE ENQUIRY

The murder squad's incident room contained a dozen pale wooden desks and off in the far right corner was Detective Inspector Ross's office, his desk positioned so that he could oversee his team beyond the half-open door. Just outside his door was Detective Sergeant Armstrong's desk, which sat currently unoccupied, as he was stood, hands thrust deep inside his tweed jacket pockets, perusing the whiteboard that ran almost the entire length of the squad room. It was currently cluttered with sheets of papers, photographs of the victims and a map of Greater London that was pinned with a variety of vibrant colours. Documents were overlapping it to such an extent that it now resembled a student's union notice board more than a working police tool.

Discouraged and exhausted Detective Inspector Ross sank back into his spring-back leather chair and stared down at his faded loafers that were definitely more of a testament to comfort than fashion. His face was pale and drawn and his trousers and shirt were crumpled as he had been up all night, going through the case notes with a fine-toothed comb. He knew that he could not afford any doubt, slip-ups or ramifications later on down the line, as the press already wanted his balls for earrings. With all the unsolved murders on his hands, both the local and national press (with their aggressive reporting) were having an absolute field day at his expense. They were as dogged and relentless as a lurcher transfixed by the scent of rabbits. The press and media were currently crucifying him and he, better than anyone, knew that it was with some degree of justification.

He sat behind a large old oak desk, which was currently cluttered with a variety of reports, printouts and discarded notes; the pieces of the jigsaw that currently were just not fitting together.

His debris-strewn desk was a vivid testament to the past few months of his working life.

Amongst the dust and clutter, a computer and printer, photocopier and two large but cheap metal filing cabinets sat, currently unused. They were lit by a harsh fluorescent strip light that sat overhead, its artificial glare, reflecting off of the office windows. As the lights cut at his eyes, the atmosphere within the room was one of quiet desperation. Sometimes he felt as though there was more chance of him understanding the new offside rule in association football than he had of cracking this particular case.

As his thoughts roamed, snippets of conversation drifted into his office from the incident room but most of it was drowned out by the clattering of keyboard keys and the incessant buzzing of the telephone lines. He could not help but to note that it felt like an asylum at times.

As he gazed out into the incident room he noted that most of the team sat at their desks, seemingly transfixed by their computer terminals. The remainder, surrounded by the fundamentals of their profession, were either writing up information on the whiteboard or conducting telephone conversions, desperately seeking the connection that would lead them to the perpetrator.

He wanted so badly to have justice for them and relief from the pain that injustice caused him. But on the surface there did not appear to be a common link as the women were all of differing ages, social status and hair types. There had to be something deeper, perhaps a personality trait or flaw that the killer had spotted, unless of course the murders were entirely at random and the women just happened to be in the wrong place at the wrong time?

Haunted by memories, he let the question float unanswered in the air.

Drumming his fingers on the desk, he returned his attention to the well thumbed photocopies of the autopsy and crime analysis reports that were sat in front of him, reading them once, before skimming through them all again, hoping to find the missing pieces of the puzzle. He just hoped that he was not being blinded by his own desperation.

He had hoped that the Police National Computer's data banks would have recognized and pinpointed similarities between the cases he was currently investigating and crimes recorded by other police forces, but he had been out of luck. In the eight months since the murders began, he had been forced to work on scraps of information. His investigation was made ever more complicated and time consuming by having to plough through stacks of false confessions that flooded in after every related news bulletin. Millions of Police National Computer data entries had been recorded and car registration numbers checked. No identifiable prints had been left at any of the murder scenes, so he was sure that the killer always wore gloves. There was a common modus operandi in all the serial killer crimes, in terms of the method of killing, but there was not much else to go on, aside from some rogue red woollen fibres that had been found at all the murder sites. Even house-to-house enquiries had elicited very little, as every householder questioned claimed to have witnessed nothing and not seen anything suspicious either on the day or on the days leading up to the murders, which was disappointing and slightly incredulous considering most of the areas concerned were supposedly under a neighbourhood watch scheme.

He assumed that the organizers were breaking several advertising laws as, 'blatantly turning a blind eye scheme' would appear to have been much more appropriate.

Over the course of the last few hours he had reread all the written statements, the autopsy reports and the Police National Computer printouts, but had failed to discover anything that had previously been overlooked. On the plus side it proved that he and his team were thorough, but on the negative side it did not move him any nearer to finding the murderer's motive. He had even resorted to covert funeral and crime scene photographs to see who attended the locations and though the press and media coverage had yielded thousands of phone calls, none had, so far, panned out.

Removing the cap on his ballpoint pen he ticked off the checklist, taking care not to jog the mug of whisky-laced coffee that sat half empty on his desk.

He felt an uneasy sense of frustration, whilst his nerves buzzed.

He had the blinds rolled up and hazy sunlight now filtered into the room, evaporating the gloom. He sat back basking in the brightness before leaning forward to take a sip of alcohol laden coffee and glance across at the photograph of his wife and two teenage daughters that sat in a silver frame upon his desk. He could not help but to feel that he had failed them. Reproaching himself, he knew full well that he had fucked it all up at the beginning of the enquiry. A suspect, who was later found to be innocent, had died as an indirect result of him stepping over the line. With hindsight he should have known that the evidence and the suspect simply did not mesh, but he had been under immense pressure from his superiors and the media to obtain a conviction, almost with any means necessary. He and his team had wasted a lot of time, wrongly identifying the suspect and building up a case against him, meanwhile giving the real murderer time and opportunity to claim more lives. He cringed inwardly at the recognition that he had embraced vengeance and called it justice. The guilt was all his. He had concentrated on the wrong man to the detriment of the enquiry and he knew that he would have to live with that knowledge on his conscience for the remainder of his days, and unfortunately for him, he was a great believer in karma.

He had been given carte blanche at the start of the murder enquiry, but that had come back to bite him on the arse big time, so he was surprised that he had remained at his rank, whilst others had taken the fall. If he screwed up again he knew that it would cost him his job, as he would be made to take early retirement or worse. He just hoped that his judgment would not be found fallible and this time his decisions untainted by impulse or desperation.

As trepidation caught him in a vice like grip, his eyes flicked back down to one of the typed documents in front of him.

He had now received back the forensic report on the Jackie Newell case.

He placed it on top of the profile from a noted criminal psychologist that stated the perpetrator was more likely than not to be a professional white male, aged twenty-five to forty-five years of age, who has above average intelligence but who will probably have had a problem with authority figures in the past. He was likely to have good knowledge of the local area though socially he would feel isolated and may have a juvenile record.

Detective Inspector Ross could not help but to think that the statement sounded as vague as that of a stage show psychic.

He was set to brief his investigation team in less than an hour and was currently unsure as to their next course of action. To make matters worse he had a press conference booked for later that afternoon and the media were currently prowling like hyenas, baying for his blood. He knew that he would have to keep his composure and be guarded in his words to them, whilst reciting an eloquent plea for vigilance and assistance.

As if sensing his spiralling mood, his phone chirped to life, snapping him from his gloomy thoughts. As he listened to the telephone ring, he absently ran his hand across the stubble of his face. He had not been home in sixteen hours and the bristles on his chin were indeed a vivid testament to that fact.

He picked up the receiver on the third ring, welcoming the intrusion into his spiralling thoughts, but waited for the other person to speak first.

"Hello, Detective Inspector Ross?"

He recognized the crime lab technician's voice immediately as he'd had many recent telephone conversations with her. He felt a wave of sudden optimism flash through his body, but it was soon to be extinguished.

"Hello Dawn. I hope you have got something positive for me as the investigation has been floundering this end."

As Dawn spoke, Detective Inspector Ross's face turned ashen in disbelief as to the information that he was receiving. His mouth went dry as his heartbeat increased. He sensed himself shudder down the earpiece as he heard the sigh in his voice, the faintest breath of regret as he spoke.

"Are you positive? What, there can be no doubt?"

He listened intently to Dawn's response as his mind attempted to put the puzzle together. He fell into a deep silence before briefly regaining his composure.

"Ok. Thank you for letting us know so quickly."

A few moments later the connection broke and a dead tone vibrated in his ear. He did not replace the telephone receiver immediately as his thoughts were currently somersaulting at the news of the latest development. The Lisa Browne murder had now been unquestionably linked to the serial killer murders. Despite the drastic change in modus operandi, the same DNA and the same rogue red woollen fibres were found on the victim's body and elsewhere at the crime scene, but at least now they had been identified.

He felt a knot of anxious tension and his heart had missed a beat at the news. He knew that in spite of the media blitz and all the precautions the police had taken, his killer had struck again, claiming victim number seven. So what had happened to change the killer's modus operandi to such an extent?

That was the million pound question, and the one, which stabbed for an answer in his mind. Were they now hunting for a type of random serial killer who changed his technique when he sought out particular victims, or did he know her?

He tried to supply an answer in his mind but failed, diverting the central murder enquiry into all manner of irrelevant paths along the way.

As he replayed the recent brief telephone conversation in his mind, his temple throbbed with pressure.

Detective Inspector Ross replaced the receiver, deliberately.

Dawn's words had sent a multitude of thoughts and emotions reeling through his brain but they now evaporated under the cloud of trepidation that settled over him. He felt fraught and anxious, more determined than ever to search out the evidence to nail the bastard who had done this.

He knew that he had now reached the darkest point in the investigation and the depth of his anguish, as the murders seemed so pointless, so random and inexplicable.

As he was getting up from his chair, the phone rang again but he chose not to answer it. He found that he was shaking and his heart was trembling like the telephone receiver in its cradle, so he needed time and space to gather his spiralling thoughts.

The phone that sat on his desk was now silent and accusatory.

Fumbling through the pockets of his jacket that hung over the back of his chair he produced a fresh sealed pack of Benson & Hedges special filter cigarettes. Breaking the seal and his resolution he fed his nicotine craving, hoping that it would now allow him to concentrate more fully.

As he drew in long hungry breaths, the cigarette worked its magic on his nicotine starved body and he felt the frustration slowing ebbing away.

He sucked the smoke deep into his lungs, feeling his heart beat faster for it…

He was still bemused by the fact that the serial killer he was seeking had changed his modus operandi so drastically, but on the plus side maybe he had finally slipped up. He just hoped that it would not remain one of those unanswered questions, like why do all call centre staff have incomprehensible accents…

He would get his squad to pool their resources and knowledge on the cases, which had up until now been treated as two separate enquiries. They would need to review the cases to date as now his stomach was churning with the uneasy feeling that the killer would strike again soon. Strangely, instead of reassuring him, the new evidence was now beginning to concern him further still.

Perhaps the fibres could prove the key to opening the case. The forensics team was now 100% certain that the rogue fibres were from a particular red patterned woollen carpet, but now would come the unenviable task of pinpointing the retail outlets and tracing their customers and staff.

The sheer scale of the project caused his mind to freeze and his body to stiffen, temporarily holding him still and breathless as his nerves tingled.

He felt ill at ease.

Talk about out of the frying pan and into the fire…

Needing to think the developments over he got up from his desk and pressed his face against the window, looking down at the car park at the rear of the police station. He watched distractedly as officers in their patrol cars either departed for their shifts or arrived at the police station escorting their prisoners.

Still deep in thought he sat back behind his cluttered desk, drumming the tips of his fingers lightly upon the surface of the polished veneer.

Feeling the onset of a headache he reached into his desk drawer to find some aspirin. Removing the packet, he popped two tablets out from the foil wrap and swallowed them with a swig of his coffee. It had gone cold and skinned over, so his throat lurched and stomach heaved at the new arrivals but with effort he managed to keep them down, though his face reddened and eyes filled up with salty tears in the process.

Even though his office door stood ajar he suddenly realized just how hot the room had become. He was momentarily puzzled. Surely the air conditioning had not broken again?

How on Earth were he and his investigation team supposed to remain focused and wide-awake when their working environment was currently akin to a Turkish steam room?

He noted that his palms were now slick with oily sweat, so plucking a couple of tissues from the box that was perched precariously on the side of his desk, he blotted the perspiration from his brow and hands before dropping the tissues into the waste paper basket next to his feet.

He switched off his computer and gently eased himself away from his desk.

Needing a break, he got up and walked out of the office, turning left to enter the main corridor. In the hallway, he carried onward before he turned right and unlocking the door, entered the gentlemen's toilet. Fortunately no one else was in the lavatory; no fellow officers to delay him in idle chatter.

Walking over to the row of three ceramic sink basins, he turned on the cold tap of the one nearest to the door. Cupping his hands, he splashed the water on to his face, reviving his senses with a shudder as a cold shiver prickled his skin. He looked up into the mirror above the sink, shocked by the reflection that stared back at him, as his guilt ridden, nicotine-starved face stared forlornly back at him from the glass. His face was prematurely furrowed, his eyes dark and complexion sallow. A light was struggling to come on in his faded eyes, to wipe away the mist that had descended on his life. It was as though his features were acknowledging his failure. Sunk in some deep moral weariness, the fatigue in his body seemed to go to the very core.

He felt a tormented man and was not sure if he could handle another year like the present one. His stomach rolled over as if he were on a roller coaster ride. He felt his chest tighten and found that he could only draw breath with effort.

He suddenly felt sick to the core of his stomach and was sorely tempted to use the air conditioning failure as an excuse to leave for the day but he knew in reality that this was never really going to be an option.

He needed to brief his team and combine the previously separate enquiries, once he'd had a chance to speak to Detective Sergeant Ryder who had been put in temporary charge of the dog-walker murder investigation.

They would need to put their respective heads together. The other members of the team could be spared the bad news for the moment, at least until this afternoon's briefing, as he sensed that their morale was already low, and having to hear that the tally was now up to seven, might crush their already fragile spirits completely.

Once again sheathed in cold sweat, he grabbed a handful of paper towels, that were the toiletry equivalent of sandpaper, from the wall dispenser and carefully patted his face and hands dry with them, before rolling them up into a semi-moist ball and sending them hurtling towards the waste bin.

He shoots, he scores…

Turning, he exited the toilet and made his way back to his office, surprised to see the corridors completely deserted. As he re-entered the incident room he saw that not much had changed during his brief absence. Most of the officers sat typing in front of their computer terminals as their screens flashed with glowing letters. The remainder seemed deep in thought or huddled in conversation, whilst scrutinizing the whiteboard, studying pages of notes before lifting the top ones to look beneath them. Well thumbed photocopies of crime analysis report forms and vehicle owners index printouts sat on the desks in front of them, surrounded by overflowing ashtrays and white polystyrene cups with varying amounts of beverages contained within them.

He cleared his throat before summoning Detective Sergeant Ryder and Detective Sergeant Armstrong into his office. They glanced at each other in an attempt to gain a clue for why they had been summoned, both equally bewildered. Nevertheless they followed him into the office and closed the door behind them.

"Take a seat."

They each pulled up a chair and sat down so that they were both facing Detective Inspector Ross. The feeling that they were regressing and had been summoned to the headmaster's office instantly flitted through both their minds, but the spell was immediately broken as he spoke.

"Okay. There has been a development that I need to update you on as it affects all of us."

As he spoke he could not help but to notice that Detective Sergeant Armstrong looked as though he too carried the weight of the world upon his shoulders. He did not look at all healthy. He looked weary. His crumpled suit, saggy jowls and the panda-like dark rings around his eyes were vivid testimony to his weariness.

Detective Sergeant Ryder on the other hand looked as immaculate as ever. Though admittedly younger than the both of them, she always presented herself as a bright young professional, svelte and spry. Today she was clad in a tight black sweater over black trousers. Most of her thick blonde hair was pulled back into a ponytail but the full fringe framed her elfin face, embellishing her beauty and drawing attention to her penetrating blue eyes and sharp cheekbones. At thirty-one years old she was still a very attractive young woman who always drew colleagues' eyes away from the matter in hand.

Although her career had been fast tracked due to the Metropolitan Police's positive discrimination policy she had more than proved her worth since her posting to Detective Inspector Ross's team. She had a keen mind and an eye for detail and had soon won over colleagues who had previously taken umbrage at her seemingly premature promotion. She had a dogged determination that sometimes bordered on bloody mindedness but in the environment they were currently operating in that was not necessarily perceived as being such a bad thing.

Detective Inspector Ross continued to fill them in on the recently taken phone call as they sat in silence, listening intently, allowing the revelations to wash over them in small waves. Detective Sergeant Ryder, in particular, realizing that this new information would radically change the course of the murder investigation that she had recently been assigned to.

Detective Inspector Ross continued to fill them in on the developments regarding the rogue red fibres that had been found at all the murder sites.

They had been identified as 100% wool from a woven Axminster carpet being sold under the name 'Cumuli Cardinal Red'. All stockists, suppliers, customers and employees would need to be traced and they would need to check with the manufacturer when that particular design of carpet went into production. They all realized that it would be a logistical nightmare and would just have to keep their fingers crossed that it had either recently been brought into range or had a limited run, but they would not hold out much hope in either regard.

Detective Inspector Ross then went on to explain that as the same DNA samples and fibre samples had been found at the dog-walker murder scene as those found in the serial killer enquiries, the investigations would now be combined and the information shared between the two enquiry teams.

He caught Detective Sergeant Ryder's eye.

"The serial killer enquiry has so far proved fruitless. Have you come up with anything new in your investigation?"

Sandra Ryder's expression remained calm and enclosed but her voice was crisp and direct as she came straight to the point.

"Yes possibly. There were no direct witnesses to the murder that have come forward as yet but a lorry driver described a guy acting suspiciously in the area, less than a half-mile from where the attack took place. The time frame would also fit. I had only just got back from interviewing him as he was driving a cargo to Rotterdam in Holland and so had only just been made aware of the publicity. He has stated that a man stepped out in front of his lorry on the morning of the incident, nearly causing what would have been a fatal accident. The man appeared completely dazed as if he were on drugs or drink, but did not appear to be injured in any way. The weird thing is that he does not appear to be like your typical addict or wino, as apparently he was immaculately groomed and impeccably dressed. The lorry driver even went so far as to describe him as 'looking like a male model from one of those poncy magazines'. (Needless to say, Vogue would not be contacting him any time soon regarding an editorial position).

The description he has given was pretty good considering he saw him only for a matter of seconds, thankfully his appearance logged in his memory due to the near accident. The guy we are looking for is big, somewhere between five feet ten inches and six feet one inch tall, clean cut with short spiky strawberry blond hair and was smartly dressed in what the witness believes was either, a dark grey or black suit and a white shirt. Someone must have seen him on the morning in question or knows who he is or where he lives. He was on foot, so is hopefully local. The lorry driver feels confident that he would recognize him again and said that he would be willing to co-operate in any identification parades we arrange or to look through photo albums of known offenders."

"Fantastic. The guy we are seeking is either a key witness or a potential suspect, so either way we need to find him as soon as possible. Once the artist's impression has been made up and enhanced, we can get it circulated to all the metropolitan police officers and get the image broadcast on all the television networks and in the newspapers. Hopefully this will be the breakthrough we have been looking for."

The thought stiffened his body, breathless as his curiosity buzzed.

Now that his serial killer cases and the dog walker murder were now undeniably linked it made the hunt for this seemingly reluctant witness ever more important. He barely dared to hope that the person they now sought may prove to be more than a witness and would actually prove to be the person that had haunted his dreams for the last eight months.

Once the police artist's impression had been made up and distributed, he would pray for a quick result.

As he turned his attention to Detective Sergeant Armstrong he felt the grumblings of heartburn begin to trouble him. He'd had to bolt his breakfast, so was now paying the price. He just hoped that he could shift it before the afternoon's press conference. At least now he would have some seemingly positive news for them, the police artist's impression and a phone number for the general public to call if they had information. He could not wait to distribute the police artist's impression to the local and national television news and the awaiting press packs. Hopefully this time the lead would result in the breakthrough that ended the murderous rampage and meant that he would hang on to his job.

"How is it going with checking out the suppliers of hunting knives?"

Detective Sergeant Armstrong's face seemed to grow heavier and darker at the posed question, almost as if it caused him pain. He inhaled deeply before answering.

"Slow. It is like looking for a needle in a bleeding haystack. I will keep on it through. I have left messages with all the local outlets to get back to me. The Internet is the problem though as you can seemingly order anything with no identification checks at all."

"Okay. Do what you can and keep me informed if we get any possible leads."

"Okay, governor."

As he answered, he pulled at his right ear with his right hand, but Detective Inspector Ross was unsure as to what that body language indicated.

Perhaps he was just being paranoid and all it signified was that Detective Sergeant Armstrong had an itch…

Both sergeants rose to return to their respective duties, leaving Detective Inspector Ross alone with his meandering thoughts. Detective Sergeant Armstrong was unmarried, but like him, his life was his work, so neither could afford failure. That led him on to thinking about his mistress and his wife, both of whom he had sadly neglected during the last eight months, the time spent on the enquiry. Feeling the sharp sting of guilt, he knew that he would be forced to make a choice once the investigation was over, if they did not make it for him, but for the moment that decision would have to be placed on the back burner. He frowned and shook his head.

As the sergeants departed to return to their assignments, Detective Inspector Ross took a deep breath, and then let it out again. He glanced down at the desk in front of him, noting the stacks of reports and messages from other police forces regarding his previous enquiries into the possibility of any similar cases within their regions. As he flicked through them he soon saw that the responses were all negative, the same with all the collated lists of possible suspects and possible witnesses.

Hopefully this new 'witness' would prove fruitful, but he just did not buy the suggestion that the person they were looking for was an alcoholic or drug addict as if he was their suspect, he was…or had been, too methodical and clever for that. That begged the question, what had spooked him so much that he had momentarily stepped out in front of a ten-ton truck before leaping back? A suicide attempt was out of the question as he had apparently jumped back as the driver had sounded his air-horn, plus the inescapable fact that he had gone on to murder an innocent woman, just moments later. Was the fact that he appeared to be so spooked the reason for the drastic change in modus operandi? In his humble opinion he would guess that it was, but he knew full well that opinions were like arse-holes, in that everybody had one. He just had to hope that this was a genuine lead and that the perpetrator was not playing games with them, as he was fully aware of the anger that was currently burning on the streets. He sat for a minute or two with his eyes closed, breathing deeply, trying to conjure in his mind's eye an image of the man they sought…but to no avail.

Opening his eyes, he picked up the witness statement that Detective Sergeant Ryder had brought in and read it through once again. It put forward so many assumptions with such vehement conviction, but he could not help but to wonder if they were all correct. How he wished that there were not so many questions on the enquiry currently without answers…

PM

His face went hard. He inhaled a deep breath and cleared his throat, before slipping out of the office to brief his assembled team.

He walked to the front of the office and stood next to the whiteboard, keen to have a visual aid for any points that he wished to make.

He stood six feet two inches tall and had a broad shouldered thick set build, so to anyone not familiar with him, he was an intimidating figure of a man who outwardly radiated the assurance that came with power. His shock of steel grey hair and piercing, almost wolverine grey eyes only added to his no nonsense demeanor.

As he addressed the assembled team, bringing them up to date with the developments, his voice boomed out across the floor freezing everyone in its wake.

As he spoke he realized that this had been the toughest test of his career to date and was well aware that any future promotional ambitions, however slight, rested on a quick result and conviction. Fail and he would remain at that rank or lower for the rest of his career. He may even be forced to take early retirement, leaving a tainted black stain on his otherwise successful career.

As he spoke his chin jerked up and his eyes blazed as the fire of determination lit his stomach with a measure of hope.

"I know that most of you have been up all night working on these cases but we must strike on these new leads whilst the iron is hot, as we need every bit of evidence that we can lay our hands on. This lowlife has had us running around like headless chickens for over eight months, so now it is time to turn the screw. I need the information on the carpet and the hunting knife as soon as possible. I need to know suppliers, start with local than go national. Check all their orders, their employees and customer records. If you get flak from any of them let me know and I will get a court order to search their records so fast it will make their heads spin. Regarding the carpet, contact the manufacturer and find out how long that design has been in production for and get a list of all their retail outlets and Internet orders for that particular design. The hunting knife will be slightly more difficult as we do not have a make just the type, but there cannot be that many local outlets, try army surplus stores and suchlike first. Check out websites as well as distributors and retail outlets. Leave no stone unturned."

He was now on a roll and produced the artist's impression that he held up for all to see.

"Also ensure that this artist's impression is distributed to every officer in the force. It is a likeness to a person that was seen in the vicinity just moments before the last murder and as such it may be the attacker or at worst a possible witness that we desperately need to trace. I have a press conference later, so the image will be broadcast, along with a direct information line. I will make sure that it gets printed in all the local papers and will release the image to the national press. Someone must have seen this guy crawl out from whatever rock it is that he is hiding, so I want him found as soon as possible."

Amongst hazy mumblings from the rank and file, the team disbanded to their duties and Detective Inspector Ross was left alone to retreat back behind his desk. He shot up a sleeve and checked his watch. There was a little less than three hours until the press conference, so hopefully there would be further developments within that time.

Reaching over he emptied the cold dregs of coffee into his waste paper basket, risking another admonishment from the cleaning staff, and poured himself a fresh hot strong cup from the percolator, before he proceeded to painstakingly go through the compilation of data, photographs, witness statements, pathology and forensic reports that were currently piled up on the desk in front of him like a literary version of Jenga.

He searched for an answer in the deep and orderly files of his mind, but for the moment, could not find one.

He knew that he needed to trust his instincts and not be dissuaded from the usual way that he tackled cases. He, more than anyone, was tired of notifying next of kin, whilst the waiting press packs bayed like jackals for his blood and news crews circled overhead like ravenous vultures.

His eyes and mind were now fully concentrated on the typed documents in front of him, so he was blissfully unaware of the hub of activity in the incident room, until the noise grew loud enough to snap him from his thoughts.

Looking up, he realized that he had never seen a team work with as much intensity, dedication and fervour as the ones on this enquiry. He felt a wave of sympathy, as they did not deserve the criticism that they had all suffered at the hands of the media. That fact would not stop him giving them a little subtle brow beating from time to time though, just to keep them on their toes as he fully believed that discipline never did anyone any harm. With all corners of the nation's media watching them intently he could not afford any more slip-ups. He sensed that he was not infallible but he hoped that the momentary pangs of renewed optimism that he was feeling were not overly premature as ultimately it would be his head upon the chopping block if the leads did not work out. As soon as scepticism reasserted itself, he shook the thought from his mind, as he knew full well that to lose hope was to admit defeat. As the old saying went 'fortune favours the brave'.

The new developments would be meaningful as long he considered them to be so.

Reaching into the inside of his jacket he removed the pack of cigarettes and lighter from his pocket and placed them on his desk whilst he smoothed back his hair that had tumbled forward. Glancing down he noted that he looked pregnant with beer, a shameful testimony to his fondness for real ale. He tugged at his belt that had inserted itself between two layers of fat, loosening the buckle to free his gut. He grimaced internally; he was dreading his next medical examination as his diet of ale, cigarettes and fast food had, for a long time, caused his doctor to tear his hair out in professional frustration.

The phone rang, shaking him from his reverie, but he did not answer it, choosing instead to watch as one of the officers in his team uncapped a black marker pen and began to write something on the whiteboard. He seemed totally oblivious to being observed, so much for coppers having a sixth sense...

With the impending press conference he attempted to gather his thoughts and went through the details that he was about to relay in his mind. The next step would be to gratify his expectations to a positive result, but he knew that he would have to first prepare the ground carefully. His faith was regained, but with such a high profile case he had to ensure that all the i's were dotted and all the t's crossed as he could ill afford any further slip-ups or ramifications later on down the line, but he felt quite confident that the previously unnerving, frustrating days were finally at an end. The sinews of his wrists were taut as he flexed and reflexed his hands in nervous anticipation. He knew that he had neither the time nor the solitude to craft the ideal speech but he felt a brief reprieve from his mounting exhaustion and a spark of hope lit his eyes for the first time in many weeks. He was no longer afraid of committing a blunder that would pitch his investigation team deeper into trouble. So, eager to rebuild his career, he stood up, straightened his tie and stole himself to address the waiting media hordes...

CHAPTER 9

A FLY IN THE OINTMENT

Karl resisted the urge to turn over onto his other side and go back to sleep. Lying under the duvet in the midst of warmth and silence he was filled with lazy contentment. The sunlight had eventually woke him up by finding a gap between the curtains and positioning itself on his face like a spotlight.

He eventually lifted his head from the pillow and glanced across at the hands of the alarm clock that regimentally tapped out the passing seconds.

He could not believe that it was now approaching 11am, as normally he was an early riser, 'up with the larks', as his dad had used to say.

Although he realized that he had now missed almost half of the day he still felt too sleepy to be discontented. There would be time for reflection later so he remained unfazed by his inertia.

Throwing the duvet off, he stood up stretched and yawned, his sleep-lagged muscles now crying out to be used after their enforced period of inactivity.

Still sotted with sleep, he padded to the heavy velvet curtains and parted them with a quick whip of his hands. Above him, the curtain rail rings clicked like a guilty Catholic's rosary beads as the sunlight flooded in to illuminate the room. He reached over to open the already ajar window a bit further and watched as the light breeze that came drifting in fluttered the net curtains like sails upon a yacht.

He padded to the bathroom, keen to relieve his aching bladder before kick starting the remainder of his day.

He slipped on a long white cotton tee shirt and made his way to the kitchen, eager for a much needed caffeine fix. He stopped in the hallway to retrieve the newspaper and an assortment of letters that sat scattered upon the doormat.

Throwing the mail onto the settee he entered the kitchen, filling the kettle and switching it on, whilst depositing a large teaspoonful of coffee and two of sugar into his favourite mug.

The pungent spicy smell of last night's lamb tikka masala and pilau rice still lingered in the air but he felt sure that it would dissipate now with the windows being fully open.

As Karl discarded the two empty foil containers along with their respective lids into the metal flip-top bin he heard the kettle switch itself off.

Reaching over to raise the kettle up he filled the mug with water and stirred the mixture until the rich coffee granules were fully dissolved, before adding a cold splash of semi-skimmed milk. He popped a couple of slices of white bread under the grill and waited until both sides were a golden bronze before garnishing them both with lashings of butter. Sometimes the simple pleasures were the best…

He carried both items into the living room, placing them onto the coffee table, before reaching for the remote control to spark the television to life.

He sat down heavily in the centre of the settee, but the mail remained unopened and paper unread as his attention was held by the news story that was currently emanating from the flashing screen, recalling memories from his own haunted past. He sat back and crossed his legs, avidly viewing the television broadcast, basking in the television coverage that he was receiving. A tall thickset police officer was giving a press conference in front of the local police station, but just then an artist's impression, very similar to his own appearance was flashed up upon the screen, giving him a start and causing him to turn the volume up a few notches. He felt his heart beating with bad news fear.

The police were looking to trace a potential witness to the local dog-walker murder and were now linking that enquiry with the serial murder cases.

He took a sharp intake of breath as if dragging hungrily on a cigarette.

His day was about to sink into melancholy.

His face drained of colour. His concentration was now blown, tearing his previous reverie to shreds.

A thought took shape in his head. Damn, why had he carried out the attack? He should have known that the woman he had seen only moments earlier was a bad omen. As the news item ended, he silently cursed his own stupidity. It was one of those things that should have never been done, akin to asking a taxi driver's opinion or having more kids than car windows…

His brain nagged at him, setting off its alarm systems and underpinning his consciousness with a general sense of foreboding.

His life now had unquestionably changed and he felt the change rolling through him as if caught up on an ocean tide.

Though still staring at the television set in disbelief, he could not sit still as he was unnerved. His heart was pounding and nerves stretched; the sweet milk of expectation had just begun to sour. He had returned to the mud of bitterness and despair as anger surged in him – boiled. He suddenly needed something stronger than coffee, so he strode back into the kitchen, re-emerging moments later with a long stemmed glass and an already opened bottle of red wine. He carried them back into the living room and sat back down onto the seat cushion that was still indented with his impression.

Pouring himself a much needed glass of Merlot, he flipped open the newspaper and absorbed the leading story. His heart missed a beat as again he was confronted by an artist's impression of his own image, and although not 100% accurate, he knew that he could still easily fall into the police net. He felt an uneasy sense of frustration and realized that drastic action would need to be taken, starting with some hair dye and the growing of some facial stubble. He just hoped that it would not be akin to shutting the stable door after the horse had bolted. Perhaps he should escape the area for a while until the media coverage waned…

He was still very rattled by what he saw and his nerves buzzed.

His innards felt weighted down as suddenly he was blasted with depression.

His previous assurance had now fallen from him like a tumbling veil and he realized that he would have to give the matter some serious consideration, as he had seriously underestimated his pursuers. He was momentarily overcome by his sense of failure, which led to an anxiety attack, his chest tightening so that he was only able to draw breath with a vast effort. Despite the efforts to calm himself, his sense of failure did not abate and his stomach rolled over as if he were plummeting down a very steep length of track. Sheathed in cold sweat the pressure on his chest increased. Each stuttering inhalation was proving to be a struggle and each exhalation an explosive wheeze. Bitterly angry, haunted memories of his childhood flashed back at him intensifying the distress he felt. A breaking inside him threatened his self-control.

Momentarily closing his eyes, as alarm flickered across his face, he strove to regain control of himself, but the sense of failure only intensified, as the thrill of his previous accomplishments now became just a distant memory.

His prospects seemed to be an empty void that sat like a looming menace, a yearning apocalypse of meaningless motions.

He knew that the odds of not ever being caught were too mathematically great to even seriously consider but he realized that if he was cautious he could postpone the event until he could go out in a blaze of glory, a final arrogant taunt to the police. He needed them to know that he meant business and could not be written off as he was enjoying the fantasy of fame. However this game eventually played out, he knew that he would not spend the rest of his natural life in prison. He would never be interred again.

Finally having regained some measure of composure, he sat back on the sofa to mull over his options as he sipped at the blood red liquid and savoured it, feeling its warmth ignite his throat and stomach.

He could only manage to draw a few shallow breaths as he reread the newspaper article, fighting back his anger as the detective in charge of the case appeared to be trying to steal his press and steal his thunder. The newspaper rattled in his hands as he read. This Detective Inspector Ross had his name and face emblazoned all over the newspaper report and he had also appeared on the television news bulletin that was just on. Karl felt his face blush with anger…this was supposed to be his story, his fifteen minutes of fame, as it was he who had done all the hard work and created the excitement after all.

He heard, in memory, the voice of his mother, so now intense anger was overtaking his usual calculated thought process. Self-pity began to spill into rage; the injustices were piling up inside him. He realized that he needed to calm down before he again did anything too rash – fame after all was such a shallow vessel.

He set aside his half finished glass of wine and got up off the settee, tossing the newspaper aside in disgust before switching off the television and making his way towards the bathroom.

A wave of nausea hit him and as he tried to gather his thoughts, an odd mixture of fear and exhilaration settled over him, a riot of emotions that he could not easily sort out.

He removed his tee shirt and hung it on the metal hook behind the door before turning on the shower attachment full force and closing his eyes whilst the warm jets of water worked their never ending magic on his taut and aching muscles, brightening the dull sheen of anxiety.

Ablutions over, he stepped out of the shower and dried his toned body briskly before putting on a pair of faded blue jeans and a white collarless granddad style shirt. He brushed his teeth and ran a comb through his hair before padding through to the living room.

He returned his empty coffee mug to the kitchen and walked slowly to the hallway. He grabbed the black New York Yankees baseball cap off of the walnut brown hat stand and placing it on his head, pulled it low over his eyes whilst tucking any rogue strands of hair beneath it.

For all he knew, the police had been keeping him under surveillance for days. Opening the door he hesitated, scanning the area outside for people skulking at the periphery of his vision.

The street outside was empty and no curtains had twitched, so he grabbed his cars keys off of the cherry veneer hall table and closing the front door behind him, stepped out into the warm summer breeze.

He walked towards the car, flared with the reflection of afternoon sunlight. He resisting the urge to break into a run, as his soles sucked at the sun soaked tarmac.

Opening the car door he sank into the vehicle like a twisting snake. He brought the seat belt across his chest and fastened it securely. Now that he was inside the car he was certain that it would not start, but it did…first time. He backed out of the driveway and drove slowly down the street, doors locked, hands clutching the wheel, sunglass covered eyes cutting in all directions, ears awaiting the inevitable wail of police sirens. His mind was twitching and he repeatedly checked the rear view mirror for pursuing vehicles, either marked or unmarked.

With the unhealthy cocktail of depression and wariness he was as shaky as a leaf in a strong wind.

He had thought that he would be safer in his car than on foot, but now sat amongst the screech of tyres, the blast of exhausts and the blare of horns sounding and engines revving in acceleration, he was not so sure.

Arriving at the local seven-eleven store he parked directly in front of the entrance whilst debating whether to drive off or get out.

As the sound of the engine cut out, concern crinkled the corners of his eyes and creased his forehead.

It was a hot day, stifling hot and humid. There were some clouds, but he felt certain that they did not contain rain.

Glancing around he noted that there was the usual collection of street life loitering about, kids skipping school and no doubt honing their shoplifting skills, a couple of winos staggering about clutching bottles of Thunderbird wine encased in brown paper bags and the obligatory drug addict (sporting long lank greasy hair, a nose ring and decked out in the deepest unrelieved black clothing) begging alongside the cashpoint machine.

No doubt outstanding pillars of the community one and all…

He mused that London with its lingering atmosphere of despair must now be considered one of the most undesirable places in England. Only in the past did it offer a hospitable place to live. Was it not Johnny Rotten who once sang about there being no future? Well how right he was as civilized behaviour and family values had been destroyed with a frightening swiftness and all that was lost could never be regained, at least not in his lifetime.

Over the noise of the street traffic, he heard the distant wail of a police siren that broke him from his trance like state and caused his heart to skip a beat, until he realized the cacophony of noise was headed away from his location.

Breaking into a sweat of fear, he gently bit down on to his bottom lip and breathed slowly and deeply, trying not to let the onlookers see how shaken he currently was.

He was confused, concerned, as he wiped sweat from his brow. He felt caught between the two proverbial stools. He knew that he was in the grip of paranoia and wondered if he was overreacting to the recent events. He wondered if he was being unduly cautious and sensitive, after all surely that artist's impression could be any one of a million guys, couldn't it?

He was initially loath to leave his sanctuary, but after a moment of uncertainty he decided to risk entering the shop, so glancing into the rear view mirror he pulled the peak of his baseball cap just that bit further down before putting on the handbrake, releasing his seat belt and swinging the car door open. Leaving it at the kerb he stepped out, and locked the door with the remote locking device he held within his increasingly sweaty grasp.

Harried by anxiety that seemed to push him forward like a rude hand, he moved across the pavement, trying not to run and thereby draw further attention to himself.

Self-absorbed and flooded with anticipation, he held his breath and ignored the curious stares from the assorted rabble, keen to avoid eye contact, as he walked across to enter the store.

Pushing through the doors that were scratched and dented, he grabbed a red plastic basket and stared straight ahead at the shelves, trying desperately to ignore everyone milling around him. He spied the toiletries section and made a beeline for it, only to find himself confronted by more choices of hair dye than in Zandra Rhode's bathroom cabinets. He eventually opted for Clairol's Nice and Easy natural medium chestnut brown and dropped the box into his basket. Passing the refrigeration section he grabbed a two-pint carton of milk and a selection of ready meals in case he was holed up for sometime to come. He popped a white medium sliced loaf on top of the items already sat in the basket and headed towards the newspaper and magazine section. Once there, much to his chagrin, he noted that a representation of his image appeared on the front pages of most of the national press. Actively fighting the urge to flee, he swallowed hard, looked straight ahead and tried to ignore the knot that was currently tying itself within his stomach. He picked up a copy of each broadsheet and tabloid, along with the last copy of the local paper and deposited the items into the basket on top of the groceries. He knew that he would have to remain alert.

Quaking with tension he headed for the till and watched as the Asian shopkeeper rang up the items before kindly bagging them for him. Slipping a twenty-pound note from his trouser pocket, he handed the money over to the cashier and waited for the change. Thankfully, no glimmer or recognition lit the shopkeeper's eyes, so he began to relax a little as he turned and exited the store, stepping back into the debris-strewn street. The wind had picked up slightly and the breeze was now spinning the discarded litter in ever increasing circles, whilst leaves fell from the nearby trees like suicidal angels.

After depositing the bags of shopping into the car, a brief and relatively unusual gap in the traffic allowed him to angle his car out from the kerbside and fall in behind a distant line of tail lights.

His brow furrowed, as if weighing something up. Then looking out of the windscreen, his eyes as blank as reflective sunglasses, he made his way slowly homeward, taking care not to draw the attention of any speed cameras or traffic police.

The sky was blue and the sun high in the sky, the city smog having apparently decided to take the day off.

Dappled with shadow, the roads weaved like serpents, whilst a cool breeze purred through the window, reviving his senses and helping to keep him alert and watchful. He glanced at his reflection in the rear view mirror, noting the haunted look in his eyes as his mind rotated through a cycle of outrage, disbelief and shock.

How he yearned once again for the cold peace of indifference.

The fabulous chest of bright dreams had been turned upside down, leaving him with no expectations.

Swamped with emotion, his lips silently worded 'I forgive you for not loving me mother', in the vain hope that inner peace would replace his current turmoil.

Tears trickled from between half closed lids as his fear soared again. He knew that he was torturing himself, but a part of him believed that he deserved to be tortured. On some subconscious level he enjoyed the drama of it all, as it made him feel alive.

Was he letting his fear run away with him again, succumbing to paranoia and just chasing his own paranoid tail?

He felt as though he was caught in a vice like grip, but before the game was over all that would change.

Approaching his locality he stopped by a pedestrian crossing. The lights were red, but there was no one stood on the pavement waiting to cross, so either the system was playing up again or the young louts up ahead (who were all attired in white logo'd baseball caps and faded, tattered blue jeans that seemed to be hanging somewhere around their knees) had been playing silly buggers. Either way – it made no difference to him. Despite the horns blaring at him from the cars stuck behind his he still waited for the crossing light to flash amber before pulling off, as he had to make sure that he was driving within the law and on no account could he afford to be spotted by an eagle-eyed traffic cop or a jobs-worth traffic warden.

He drove cautiously but still with the expectation of relentless pursuit, which thankfully did not occur. Fearing his return home, he was almost certain that his access would be blocked by the sudden arrival of swarms of police cars, but none were in sight as he steered homeward…

Karl drove up the driveway to his home and shut off the engine. He undid his seat belt, opened the car door and got out. He was in the process of locking the car door when he saw a shadow move nearby. His heart skipped a beat, bringing the hairs on the back of his neck to attention, until he realized that it was just a grey tabby cat which had just jumped the garden wall and was now contentedly lapping droplets of rainwater off of the lawn's blades of grass.

He felt the relief and was surprised, surprised by how much comfort was generated.

He knew that he was letting his paranoia get the better of him again, but his mouth still went dry and his heartbeat increased.

He grinned at his own anxiety, acknowledging his own failings. He felt stupid and careless, although he knew that in reality he was neither.

He drew a deep breath which he exhaled seconds later with a shudder before walking on towards the front of his house.

He inserted his key into the front door lock and opened the gateway to his abode. Entering and closing the door behind him, he made his way through the long hall, to the kitchen and deposited the shopping bags onto the kitchen table.

He felt slightly more comfortable with the proof that his instinctive and fascistic ability to organize and control his environment had not entirely left him.

Helping himself to a second glass of red wine, he removed the assorted newspapers from their bags and began to skim through the varying headlines, half afraid to see their contents. The publicity had now become a torch for him – a light in his world of darkness and despair...

His feelings were currently a mixed bag of emotions as on one side he was tingling with anticipation, basking in the coverage, waiting to see what names the papers would be coining for him today but on the other side he felt consternation over the mass publication of his likeness. Fortunately the latter problem could be easily rectified given a little time and creative imagination.

Once he had speed read through the glaring headlines he sat reading the full articles with slow deliberation, seeking to elicit how much the police now actually knew.

As he absorbed the printed words, his broad face clouded with concern.

He found that the newspaper reports were as frightening as they were uplifting, his emotions spinning as inner turmoil simultaneously touched his heart and mind, veering them between euphoria and despair.

He had always realized that he would attract a lot of media attention but it had been very different from what he had anticipated as it appeared to be focusing more on the police's failings rather than his own unique merits. A cold tide washed through his heart. He did not count on being so largely misunderstood by the press but their ignorance was a bliss that meant further women would die.

Trapped in a vicious circle, he felt like he was upon an emotional rollercoaster. On one hand there was a great deal of fear in London and it had been over eight months without the sniff of an arrest, so he felt that he was entitled to feel a warm glow and sense of achievement, but on the other hand he realized that without further murders his notoriety would wane. He craved the publicity, as he had always wanted to be somebody, to achieve something, to prove his parents wrong…

His skin tightened as his nerves buzzed at their memory, as they were the figures that sought him in his nightmares, the inevitable pursuers through his corridors of dreams and into the maze of his mind. They had taught him how to hate and how to hurt…

He did not realize that he was holding his breath until he exhaled hard with relief.

Forcing the thoughts from his mind, he reached over for the remote control. He switched on the portable television, which sat upon the kitchen unit, to receive the latest news bulletins. As he did so, a useless anger rose within him but he felt no remorse, he never had.

Unknowingly the reports would feed his injured mind and stoke the fantasies of the sweet avenging angel inside him, seeking to avenge the hurt. His faith was regaining all that was lost in the savage therapy of quiet rage and periodic violence whilst his desires felt so hot that he felt burnt in the flames of them. His blind anger hotter than ever as his memory pulled up visions from the past. The simmering anger of his childhood and adolescence began to swell within him and he involuntarily clenched and unclenched his fists, yearning to strike something or someone.

He felt shaken by his lack of self-control, and into his mind sank a foreboding vision.

He had to kid himself into believing that life had a purpose and one that was worthy of his struggle. To evade the ghosts that would jar him from his sleep to invade his waking thoughts and dreams. He took a deep breath as he sank into semi-awareness, letting the thoughts wash over him and feeling a strange but familiar resentment.

No old friends saw him and he had no family of which to speak. His whole world was like a corporate operation, a trigger happy conglomerate where individuals were expendable cannon fodder.

As he once again glanced down at the various editions of the newspapers in front of him, the face of one unforgotten ghost (his last victim) would rock him from his trance.

His mouth began to dry as he steeled himself to continue reading.

Childish self-pity welled up within him as he sat motionless for a minute or two with his eyes closed, breathing deeply, rifling his mind trying to conjure in his mind's eye, an image of a better time.

Finally admitting defeat, with teeth clenched so tightly that his jaw muscles twitched continuously, he read the stories, scanning the contents before him with the eyes of a critic.

As a mixture of rage and terror manifested itself within him, he skipped past photographs to search for the details of the officer that was currently in charge of the investigation.

They would need to chat as everyone knew that rubbing a wound retarded its healing. He would pay the officer a visit and quench his curiosity.

During the course of his reading he had been unable to breathe, though he had thought he would be prepared. The articles had been so inadequate; they had not captured his intelligence or cunning, but he knew that he was now the hunted as opposed to the hunter…

A breaking inside him threatened his self-control; he would have to get their faces and words out of his mind.

Bending forward in the chair, covering his face, shuddering, he muffled his voice into his cupped hands.

'Damn them. Damn them all to hell.'

Rage gnawed within him, biting deep enough to rouse him from his long trance of self-pity and abject despair.

After a moment or two he lowered his hands from his face and sat up straight again to focus on the way ahead.

He seethed with a sense of injustice and treachery; he felt that there was wrongness with the world, far beyond the mere cruelty of it.

Never mind the media, as when the time was right he would have his own revelations to make and truths to reveal. He was halfway through his journey so there could be no going back.

He wanted them all to feel the pain that he had…

LATER

Karl had finally calmed down into a disgruntled misery and laid in absolute silence along the settee for the remainder of the afternoon.

He knew that he would need to remain guarded but was unsure of how to eliminate the blanket of suspicion that he may yet fall under.

As he drew in a deep breath he shuddered inwardly at the realization that perhaps he and Detective Inspector Ross would need to get better acquainted...

CHAPTER 10

THE ENCOUNTER

The public house opposite the police station was filled with the usual crowd; tired officers closing the day off with a much-needed tipple after work.

The officers, who had previously been loud and raucous, either began speaking in hushed tones or else fell completely silent as Detective Sergeant Sandra Ryder walked in. She had been propositioned and had rejected the advances of most of them, even the married ones, so their reaction to her entrance came as no surprise.

Boys will be boys…

She'd had time to shower and change her clothes after work, so she was now 'dressed down' in a pair of faded blue drainpipe jeans and a black baggy sweatshirt.

Her long flaxen hair, still slightly damp, was worn loose and hung down over her shoulders, obscuring her breasts. Her eyes had been darkened with kohl and mascara and her lips glossed red with lipstick.

Perching herself upon a bar stool she caught the bartender's eye and gestured for her usual drink. He poured the house double vodka into the tumbler and added a slice of lemon and some rapidly thawing ice cubes for good measure, before placing in onto the bar.

Reaching into her handbag, to remove her purse, she slid a ten-pound note across the bar to him and waited for the change.

As she surveyed the scene, she noted that the lighting was discreet and the décor at best could only be described as strictly functional. The walls were painted in a shade of green that made her feel slightly nauseous. Aside from the close proximity to work she had no idea why she went there, but it was what she liked to do when working on a particularly troublesome case.

Well that, and the burden of loneliness.

Although now officially off duty, jumbled thoughts from the investigation still ricocheted through her head.

As she sat staring down into her glass of clear liquid, she clinked and rattled the ice in the tumbler, subconsciously trying to block out the pounding jukebox music.

Gary Glitter was enquiring if she wanted to be in his gang…but as he was now fat, bald and currently working his way through the pedophile capitals of the world, she silently decided to decline his kind offer.

She drank the two-shot glass of vodka straight down before catching the bartender's eye and gesturing for a refill.

Much to the chagrin of other officers already stood waiting at the bar to be served she received her drink first …being able to paint on a smile had its uses.

Beside the bar to her right, stood a tall, strikingly attractive man with thick chestnut brown hair and clad in a black shirt with extended cuffs that reminded her of raven's wings. His large blue eyes gave him the innocent demeanor of a choirboy, whilst his smile was easy and despite herself she felt flushed with girly excitement. He seemed sort of kind and friendly and the hairs on the back of her neck began bristling with anticipation.

He was standing alone and wore no wedding band so hope momentarily skipped across the surface of her heart.

With her luck in the romance stakes, he would undoubtedly turn out to be gay or have more baggage than a Boeing 747.

If not, she just hoped that their thoughts were running on precisely the same track.

She was not naïve and knew that love was always over the next morning.

She was almost face to face with him, searching his eyes, which were like deep unexplored oceans.

His magnetic eyes drew her in and momentarily she felt lost as a knot of nervous anticipation grew in her stomach.

She risked a smile towards him, which he reciprocated.

A flurry of brief smiles was always the safest icebreaker…

On Karl's part this blonde's spectacularly long legs and pert bottom had engaged his interest and were about to seduce him into conversation.

Karl felt a flush of anticipation as the woman next to him was quite startlingly beautiful, her features exquisite and her figure sublime.

As he looked across at the woman, he could not help but to note that her eyes were like calm pools in which he saw humbling depths of acceptance and a kindness that shone like moonlight upon water. He caught a slight smell, the tiniest hint of perfume, although he was not experienced enough to recognize the scent.

Strangely, although he did not know her, he felt a connection that had eluded him for so long. Without struggle or determination, this strange development temporarily stripped off the armour of indifference in which he had previously clothed himself. His hate had momentarily drifted like a forlorn spirit to be replaced by a curious sensation in his chest, a tightness that was both painful and exhilarating.

Although he was yet to touch a drop of alcohol he felt half nauseated, half out of his mind – but more alive than he had been in his entire life.

He momentarily averted his gaze from her eyes to catch the bartender's attention.

"Can I have a glass of your house red?"

He paused momentarily before deciding to take the plunge and rather boldly edged himself towards her.

"May I buy you a drink?"

Although Sandra still had a yet untouched double house vodka set down in front of her, she did not want to risk him seeking companionship elsewhere.

She was feeling lonely and tonight she needed someone.

"Thank you. I will join you with the house red, if that is okay?"

With the drinks order now having been placed, the bartender turned his back towards them and after the chinking of glasses and the popping of a cork, returned to them with two glasses of deep claret.

"That will be £4.40, please."

Karl flipped open his tan leather wallet and removed a five-pound note, which he proceeded to slide across the counter to the waiting barman.

"Stick the change in the charity box."

"Thank you, Sir."

Sandra gave him a smile and a slight nod to acknowledge his kindness, before feeling the need to break the ice further.

"Thanks for the drink. I haven't seen you in here before – are you just passing through?"

"No. I'm relatively local but just not much of a pub person as a rule. They tend to be too smoky and too noisy. I prefer my entertainment slightly more cultured."

He instantly regretted his last sentence the moment that it had left his lips as he did not want to appear too snobby or pretentious.

Thankfully his faux pas seemed to go unrecognized by his new friend as she smiled back at him, albeit fleetingly.

They exchanged names and the usual pleasantries for the next few minutes, each trying to listen intently to each other's replies, whilst vainly attempting to block out the infernal din resonating from the various tables within the public house.

Both parties, although they had just met, were feeling a mutual attraction.

Karl was feeling exhilarated, yet fearful of these new unfurling emotions, and at one point let out an almost childlike sigh.

He felt a satisfaction that he had never experienced before, a wild glee that simultaneously thrilled but confused him. His heart was currently beating so fiercely within his chest cavity that his vision momentarily blurred with the hard driven surge of blood. He took a deep breath in an attempt to recapture the composure that his body seemed to be rapidly losing.

Sandra, for her part too, was experiencing a fluttering of the heart. It had been a long time since a regular guy had taken an interest in her. Regrettably, married policeman and boozed up criminals tended to be her usual fan base.

As far as she knew, he might be a criminal with a list of heinous crimes on his police record, but he did not look like a criminal and did not sound like one, but she knew better than anyone, that no man was ever what he seemed.

As the evening progressed Sandra made even more of an impact on him and the emotions that Karl was now experiencing felt more real than anything else in his life had previously.

With the traumas of his past and the regular nightmares from his childhood always lurking somewhere deep within the walls of his mind, he wished that he could be lost forever in this moment.

The more he studied her, the more beautiful he realized she was – her long blonde hair shone as if were wheat basking in the golden haze of the sun, her skin smooth like alabaster, her lips full and ruddy and her huge blue eyes as alluring as lapis lazuli.

He had previously been incapable of knowing such common human emotions as passion and promise, but now for the first time in his life, he felt totally drained of anger, but was still unsure as to whether he trusted his self-control.

Briefly lost in his eyes Sandra felt a knot of nervous anticipation grow within her chest.

Due to the surrounding noise continuing unabated they had subconsciously edged closer together, now almost whispering in each other's ears.

Sandra laughed softly, pleasingly, and as she spoke her fluid voice sounded to Karl like a heavenly choir of angels.

Her features so fragile, throat so slender and shoulders so delicate, that the finest Italian craftsman could have easily sculpted her.

As they spoke, Karl sensed a connection, unexpectedly for him, and wondered whether his future could now be changed for the better. He knew that his own life was as hollow as an empty shell; the tortured spirits that soiled him and the bruised stare of hurt and loneliness confronted him daily.

For a brief moment he had tumbled to a darker place within his mind...

Sensing his distraction, Sandra glided her hand over Karl's as she spoke and the gentleness of her fingertips against his skin, the light in her eyes and the tender lilt in her voice all marked her out as a woman of great compassion, and soon brought his thoughts back into the light.

Karl took a deep breath, as he did not want to lose a grip on this reality.

To his own surprise, a flicker of sexual interest was blossoming inside him, and he had forgotten how good that feeling was.

The buzz of voices around the bar at the back picked up again, having temporarily died down for a while.

Karl was becoming overwhelmed with a desire to kiss Sandra but his internal alarm bells rang a little at this, but then he became more accepting, feeling the airy freedom of displacement. For once he enjoyed not being in control.

Due to the continuing chorus of increasingly inebriated patrons, the public house was no longer proving to be a convivial location for a romantic interlude.

Sandra – who was becoming evermore fractious with the resonating background noise decided to act first.

"Karl, do you fancy grabbing a bite to eat?"

The use of his name immediately drew a net of significance around them...

Her eyebrows raised quizzically when she spoke, almost urging the response to be a positive one.

Karl had not yet dined and had been thinking along the same lines himself (but was reluctant to appear too forward).

"Yes, that would be great. As this is your neck of the woods, can you suggest anywhere?"

"There is a nice little Chinese restaurant just a few minutes walk from here.

It is not too pricey and the food is to die for. That is, if you like Chinese cuisine?"

"It's my favourite food," he lied.

"That's settled then."

As they downed the last of their respective beverages, a thunderbolt of a reality check hit Sandra.

Although most of her colleagues had long since departed the hostelry, some still remained.

Despite the fact that she had not openly lied about her profession to Karl, she feared that he may not quite see it that way. In her defence though, they had only just met and the term 'civil servant' did cover a wide multitude of sins.

She may never see the guy again after tonight, so there was little point in perturbing him unnecessarily. There was nothing wrong with a little white lie when told for the good of all parties concerned, surely?

As they headed for the exit, Sandra kept her eyes low and pace brisk, and was fortunate enough to escape without acknowledgement.

Either the remaining officers had been too inebriated to notice her departure or their noses had been put firmly out of joint by her now leaving with a civilian.

Either way, she was grateful for small mercies.

After a brief stroll under the sun's dying embers, they arrived at the Jade Garden.

Sandra noted that Karl had taken up the position nearest the road whilst they had walked to the restaurant and now he stood holding the restaurant door open for her.

She had not experienced courtesy like that since the eighties. Perhaps chivalry was not dead and perhaps love did not have to be over the next morning…

She would have to try to hang on to this one.

A small Chinese waitress approached them, smiling hospitably, before eyeing Karl.

"Could we have a table for two please?"

"Certainly Sir, if you would both like to follow me."

Both Karl and Sandra did as they were instructed and found themselves being led to a discreet corner table set into a little alcove.

Obviously the waitress had assumed that romance was on the agenda and so had given them the restaurant's most romantic spot.

Both Sandra and Karl felt a little uneasy about the romantic setting but both were too polite to point out the error to the waitress, who after all had only been trying to help Cupid upon his merry way.

The restaurant seemed somewhat bigger on the inside than it had done on the outside, so had obviously been based on the blueprint for the Tardis.

The lighting was subdued and tea light candles sat upon the table giving off both a romantic but also a welcoming and inviting feel. The decoration and furnishing were rich in colour and texture and added to the homely feel.

Menus were handed to both Sandra and Karl in turn, which they were left to peruse whilst the waitress attended to the restaurant's other patrons.

She reappeared minutes later, eager and attentive.

"Are you ready to order yet?"

It was Sandra who spoke up first.

"Could I have the gourmet mixed hors d'oeuvres for starters, followed by sweet and sour pork balls, special chop suey and special fried rice? Thank you."

"Would you like anything to drink?"

"I will have a white wine spritzer please. Thank you."

"And for you, sir?"

"I will have the same please. Thank you."

"Very good, sir."

The waitress gathered up the menus and disappeared towards the kitchen area.

It was Sandra who broke the momentary silence.

"Was that just a case of great minds thinking alike or could you not decide for yourself?"

Karl laughed, "Perhaps it was a little of both?"

The conversation then flowed unabated, both thankful to have left the noise pollution of the hostelry far behind.

Moments later the waitress re-emerged with the drinks order, but seeing that they were now deeply engrossed in flirtatious conversation she made her appearance fleeting.

When the meals arrived they were delicious, the pork succulent, the batter crisp and fresh, whilst the rice and noodles were prepared to perfection.

Both Karl and Sandra were feeling that the other was an exquisite dinner date, hence new sensations and emotions were now bubbling within each of them.

Throughout the meal the conversation never faltered, Karl was charming and attentive, Sandra witty and captivating. Each with so much natural charm and charisma that they found they were connected on so many levels, hence all evening the conversation had flowed easily between them.

It was almost like Fate had brought them together, but it had yet to be decided if it were the Gods or the Devil who was dealing their respective hands.

Karl forever found himself gazing into Sandra's face, delighting in her obvious beauty, but at the same time searching her eyes for her soul's darkest secrets.

Sandra, for her part, was doing pretty much the same to Karl, but neither one of them was currently coming up with the answers they sought.

The alcohol that they had both consumed in the pub and now at the restaurant had relaxed them both to the extent that inhibition was minimal; hence the flirtatious behaviour had begun to step up a gear.

Sandra tossed her long blonde mane away from her shoulders, sensing that she looked positively radiant in the flickering candlelight.

Karl felt utterly bewitched and silently prayed that this night would never end.

Unfortunately the time of the restaurant's closure was drawing rapidly upon them, as out of the corner of their eyes they spied chairs being placed on top of the tables and tired looks from the hovering waitress.

Karl motioned for the bill and when it arrived he dug a credit card from his wallet, waving away Sandra's protestations to pay her half.

Once the credit card was returned to Karl and a generous gratuity left, they departed into the cool crisp night air.

Sandra leant forward and kissed Karl tenderly on the cheek.

"Thank you for the meal. It was lovely and I had a truly wonderful time."

Without knowing it, his fate and hers were now inextricably linked.

Fleetingly lost in the moment, a knot of nervous tension grew in Karl's throat. He reached out and gently placed his hand on the side of Sandra's face, then leaning forward, kissed her tenderly on the lips. He felt a little ashamed of his excitement but then Sandra leant forward to kiss him again and their bodies came together, softly and slowly at first, and then completely. Her body felt warm and deeply contented and when she eventually pulled away her eyes were full of promise – perhaps eager to enact her fantasies upon him?

"Would you like to come back for a nightcap?"

It was an invitation that Karl could not possibly resist.

"That would be great. Do you live far from here?"

"I live just a few streets away. As it's a nice night, we could walk, unless you would prefer to get a taxicab?"

"No, I am fine with walking, if you are."

In truth Karl was glad of the opportunity to stretch his legs and a moonlit stroll with someone of such exquisite beauty could hardly be regarded as a chore.

The moon up above was full and shining bright, as if a spotlight on their act.

They momentarily stopped walking to look up at the sky.

Sandra as though sensing herself in the starring role slipped her arm through Karl's and snuggled into him closer as they walked.

A gentle warmth ran through her as they did so.

The streets were almost empty so the sound of their shoes on the paving stones echoed eerily through the night air.

As they passed a row of obviously well tended gardens, the scent of freshly mown lawns mingled with the scent of flowers and filled the air with a fragrant perfume, temporarily masking the usual London smog and the greasy scent of the nearby take-away restaurants.

Quarter of an hour later, they had arrived at their intended location.

It was a mid-terrace house which was painted a gleaming white.

Sandra opened the gate to her property and proceeded up the garden path to her previously unlit home, but which was now illuminated by the outside security light that shone bright, momentarily dazzling them both.

Sandra reached into her handbag for her front door key, inserted it into the lock and upon turning it, the door sprang open as their black silhouettes stood half framed in the doorway.

She flicked on the light switch so that the hallway was now illuminated.

Although not furnished to quite the same standard as Karl's abode, it was still tastefully decorated.

"Don't stand on ceremony. Come on in."

There was a sexy, smoky quality to Sandra's voice now that prickled Karl's skin, not to mention his interest still further.

He pushed through the front door and entered into the long hallway which was warm and well lit.

Sandra indicated to a room on the left.

"Make yourself at home, whilst I'll go and grab the wine."

Sandra departed, laughing softly as she saw Karl struggling to dislodge the multitude of cushions from her settee, to find an unobstructed space to sit.

As Karl looked around the living room, he saw that it had a refined, almost classical air to it. On the magnolia painted walls hung simple framed black and white photographs, shots of brooding skies and rain soaked landscapes.

Karl thought it was odd that the pictures were free of animals or human figures.

By stark comparison, the floor was carpeted in a lush red weave and the furniture consisted of a large burgundy suite with very ornate scroll arm designs and solid wooden feet.

Sandra reappeared moments later, clutching an already de-corked bottle of a fine Merlot and two long-stemmed crystal wine glasses.

A momentary wave of sorrow fell across Karl's blue eyes but soon vanished, without Sandra noticing.

Perhaps desire and despair did walk hand in hand after all?

Sandra poured the wine until the blood red liquid had filled both their glasses. As she handed one to Karl he accepted the drink with a smile and once he had savoured it, a nod of appreciation.

He had not tried this particular vintage before so was keen to experience the wine fully, settling the wine on his tongue and breathing in to release the flavour and swilling it gently around his mouth before swallowing. The velvet liquid warmed his throat instantly and lingered on his tongue as he spoke.

"It is a lovely place you have got here. You have decorated it well."

"Thank you. It still needs a bit of work, but I am relatively happy with it thus far."

Pleasantries over, she took a seat next to Karl on the settee. Reaching over she sparked the compact disc player to life and much to Karl's chagrin, Mick Hucknell's whining voice began to resonate from the speakers.

He sensed that unless this was a compilation CD, the night could now feel very long indeed.

Alas, his worst fears were realized when track two kicked in…

He could never quite fathom the affection that women felt for Simply Red when most men would rather walk barefoot through miles of broken glass than have to endure their attempts at 'music'.

Karl noted that Sandra had a 3-disc CD player, so if Meatloaf or Cher came on next, he would have no option but to make his excuses and leave.

Sandra was gorgeous and fantastic company, but surely there had to be limits to his or any man's endurance…?

Whilst attempting to block out the aural graffiti currently assaulting his taste and senses, Karl initiated some conversation in an attempt to steer the previously romantic evening back on track.

His heart was slightly trembling as he watched her changes of expression and listened intently to her lilting tone, which was a unique combination of beauty and rhythm.

He watched her in relative silence, looking tenderly into that beautiful and delicate face, realizing that she would never know his inner turmoil and the sadness of his ravaged spirit. Maybe they were wounds that would never heal?

Sandra slipped forward a little and began to kiss him tenderly, affectionately, before they kissed more heavily, deeper, touching and murmuring to one another. Karl adored her sweet kisses and gentle touch and found himself moaning contentedly as she sucked on his tongue before rolling her own tongue slowly around his mouth, their tongues clashing like rapiers.

He responded in kind, showing her sensuous mouth the same amount of attention, shedding his world-weariness whilst sating his thirst for love.

He held her body tightly to him, losing himself in the moment.

The countless secrets temporarily evaporating as their respective hearts fluttered as if tiny butterflies.

Sandra was the mistress of the practiced flirt and had definitely netted her catch on this occasion.

Slipping her arm around his body she blew lightly into his ear before flicking her tongue rapidly inside as if a striking serpent.

Karl's breathing began to get heavier and more irregular, so sensing his arousal Sandra began to drape herself over him, moulding herself into his body, a feline, elegant movement and madly seductive.

Karl ran his hands over her exposed flesh, the skin smooth and taut beneath his fingertips, her face flawless.

Love was a miracle that temporarily had defeated his ghosts.

Karl felt keenly the fragmentation of his life and just hoped that what could possibly develop into a long and fruitful relationship was not now going to become a short, intense and soon-to-end moment of out of control lust.

He could feel her long thick eyelashes vibrating gently upon his neck, triggering a tingling sensation in his loins. One of his hands reached for her buttocks, caressing the pert contours, whilst the other slipped around her waist before climbing her slender back.

Sandra's head was still resting on Karl's shoulder, her body sculptured into his so that he could feel the rhythm of her heart, which was currently beating with all the intensity of a tribal drum.

Her hair and body were glistening so provocatively that his body ached all over with desire.

He began to run his fingers through her now tousled mane, his eyes half-closed, still surprised by the feelings that she had given him.

The fragrant scent of her perfume now hung in the air, floating into his lungs like a potion of love.

He felt mesmerized as if under an enchantress's spell.

Sandra was now running her slender fingers across his inner thigh, just skirting the prominent bulge that she could see had arisen nearby. The other hand she placed around Karl's slim but toned waist. Now fully excited she had become sexy and flirtatious. Her fingers caressed the swollen spot between his legs as her tongue tasted his mouth, stifling his stuttering gasps, whilst enhancing his desire.

He gazed at her, full of lust. His attention drifted down to Sandra's breasts where the outline of her nipples protruded deliciously from beneath her top.

His hand slipped between her thighs, rubbing against the wetness from her pussy, arousing her even more.

She pressed her breasts against his chest, her arms holding him tightly. His hot constricted breath touched her skin and she raised her head to meet his eyes, whilst his erect lightning rod prodded at her thigh.

They looked at each other longingly before putting their lips together, kissing violently, passionately, and each seeking to devour the other.

Their desire was as if a raging fire burned inside them.

Karl forced his tongue into Sandra's mouth, momentarily sucking her breath from her, but still unable to stop the tingle of excitement that currently enveloped her body. She paused to pull her sweatshirt over the top of her head exposing her naked breasts. She then began to unbutton Karl's shirt, exposing his naked torso to her cool gaze. Grabbing his hand, determination in her eyes, she led him to the bedroom.

The bed was a king-size, the covers turned down exposing red satin sheets.

They both removed the remainder of their clothes without ceremony, leaving them strewn upon the bedroom floor, tidiness being the least of their current considerations.

They lay naked, side by side on the bed, looking into each other's eyes as their hands explored the contours of each other's bodies.

Sandra caressed his twitching rod, keen to keep it at its current firmness, lubricating it slightly with one of the sensual oils that sat upon her nightstand. She passed the bottle of massage oil over to Karl and then lay back as he gently massaged her, gliding his hands over her exposed breasts and stomach, before caressing downwards, towards the valley between her legs. He slid first one, then two fingers inside her, stimulating her arousal still further. Satisfied that she was now ready, he lowered himself between her legs, glancing up as he positioned himself between her quivering thighs.

A low moan of pleasure escaped from Sandra's lips, her voice coloured with arousal as his tongue explored her moist cavern. Parting her pubic hair he began to nuzzle at her throbbing bud.

She lay back with her eyes closed, not wanting to interrupt the ripples of pleasure that were beginning to wash over her. Drifting into sensual reverie, she stretched out her sleek body, welcoming the pleasure whilst inhaling the scent of her own musk. As the tremor of orgasm thrashed through her body she pressed deeper into his face, yearning for his mouth and tongue to explore her juicy lips still further.

After feeling, tasting the orgasm wash over her, Karl shifted his position and slid his throbbing and twitching rod inside her heavenly lips, feeling his long shaft fill and stretch her. As he thrust inside her, he nibbled at her neck and at the top of her shoulders, nipping them at first then biting harder as the pleasure intensified. He kissed her longingly, hungrily, biting her lip and sucking her tongue as he ejaculated inside her. Feeling the hot climax, Sandra let out a contented purr of pleasure whilst basking in the haze of sexual contention.

Karl too was feeling sated and leant forward to kiss her lightly on her lips.

They lay entwined as sleep overtook them, casting them adrift into their own subconscious, the day slipping into oblivion…

CHAPTER 11

THE NEXT DAY

Karl awoke as sunlight filtered in through the partially opened curtains, bathing his face in light as if he were under a stage spotlight.

Sandra stirred next to him but did not awaken.

Jewels of perspiration were sparkling on her naked flesh, adding a silk like sheen to her gloriously sleek body.

Karl felt exhausted but found that he could not fall back to sleep. He found himself restlessly moving, trying to mould his body into the mattress that now seemed so hard and unyielding.

As he looked around to survey the room, he felt a cold coil of remorse spring from his chest. Now that he had finally experienced genuine emotion he yearned to end his anguish and terminate the nightmares that now constantly ripped him from his slumber. He felt a mixture of emotions and wondered if the wounds to his soul would ever be truly healed as his heart had never truly had a place to belong. Experiencing an overload of feelings, his usual ordered thoughts now just came randomly tumbling out so he realized that he would need to get a grip on himself before Sandra awoke.

Finally the anxiety yielded, falling away from him like an unbuttoned shirt.

He was still hot, sticky and sweaty from the previous night's exertions so he padded naked to the bathroom. He ran himself a bath, adding some of Sandra's sweet almond bath oil, before slipping gently in. He lay in the water, luxuriating, letting the small rolls of waves wash over his willing body until he felt fully relaxed and at peace. Only then did he begin to gently scrub his body clean.

Sandra opened her eyes and stirred from under the bed sheet, her hair hanging about her shoulders. For a moment she wondered where the sound of water was originating coming from.

Still sleepily contented she climbed out of bed, strolled over to the curtains and whipped them open to allow the rest of the morning sunshine in, the light so harsh that it made her blink.

Reaching up to the hook on her bedroom door, she slipped on her black satin dressing gown before quickly running a brush through her hair, reinvigorating the fullness and body that it had shown the night before.

Walking across the room, she opened the bedroom window a little further so that a cool breeze now fluttered the net curtain like a sail, before softly caressing her skin as if it were a gloved velvet hand.

Two crystal long stemmed wine glasses sat, perched precariously, upon her dressing table. She gently lifted one to her lips, sipped at the red nectar and savoured it. Her face crinkled with pleasure, a combination of the Merlot and the floating memories of the night before.

She just hoped that he was as dashing in the cold light of day as he had been with her wine goggles on…

She could hear the bath water now being sucked down the plughole before it omitted a loud and seemingly satisfied belch.

Karl emerged, somewhat sheepishly, clad only in a bath towel that was wrapped around his waist.

"Good morning."

"Oh. Good morning. Did I wake you?"

"No, I don't think so. Did you enjoy your bath?"

"Oh, yes. Thanks. I hope that you didn't mind me using it, but I didn't like to wake you to ask."

"God, no, it's not a problem at all. Did you sleep well?"

"Yes, like the proverbial log. And you?"

"Ditto. Would you like a coffee?"

"I would love one. Thanks."

Sandra made her way to the kitchen as Karl entered the bedroom to get dressed.

As she ran the cold tap to fill the kettle, she suddenly realized that she didn't know how he took his caffeine fix.

"Do you take milk and sugar?"

"White with two sugars, please."

"Okay."

When Sandra returned to the bedroom minutes later, Karl was dressed simply in his white linen shirt, open at the neck and what were once crisply pressed black trousers but which now held a concertina effect from where they had lain discarded on the floor, a victim of the previous night's activities.

Sandra studied him as she entered.

His hands, large with slender fingers, lay quietly on his lap as he leaned forward on the bed, his expression a studied mask of confidence.

Sandra passed the steaming mug of coffee to him, which he accepted with a smile, before she took a seat on the bed next to him.

Both wished to say something exciting and erudite but a slight case of uncertainty and embarrassment had now begun to affect both their mindsets.

Two questions were stabbing like daggers within their minds.

The initial surge of excitement had now been subsided as reason returned.

Each was wondering where, if anywhere the relationship (IF there was actually a 'relationship') went from here. And secondly, what feelings had the other towards them.

Each was now realizing that they would be treading the 'morning after' minefield until one of them had the courage to lay their respective cards on the table.

Karl smiled before glancing around the room, hoping to notice something that would give him a nudge in the right direction. Alas, with the exception of a solitary black and white photograph of some unspecified country landscape that hung on a simple white wall, no personal affects, flowers or ornaments were on display, hence the room revealed very little about its occupant and therefore provided extremely little in the way of a conversational ice-breaker.

Noticing Karl surveying her bedroom but not commenting on it, Sandra felt the need to defend her corner. For some reason it mattered to her what opinion he was currently forming of her and her tastes.

"I have not long moved in, so the décor is a tad sparse."

"I think it's nice–crisp, clean and very serene."

Sandra felt relieved by the response.

Karl too was relieved that he had triumphed over caution as he had wanted it out of his head.

They sipped at their coffees, exchanging quips and banter, the air a lot easier now.

As Sandra studied him, the attraction that she had felt the previous day was still as strong. The touch of this sexy looking guy definitely did something to her. Her mind raised the question that he could be a rogue or a villain, but the sensation between her legs ultimately urged her to reach a very different conclusion. The feelings of pure lust that, previous to last night, had been long buried, flashed once again into her consciousness. This was someone that she wanted to date again and the sooner the better.

Momentarily taken aback by her carnal craving she felt herself redden as a glow of embarrassment lit her cheeks.

With a mild glint in her eye, she stuttered an excuse about grabbing a quick shower and walked quickly out of the room before the urge to throw herself on him resurfaced again.

Karl's gaze was fixed on her as she left, unsure of what to make of her sudden departure and now wondering if he had outstayed his seemingly previous welcome.

Despite his confusion, Karl decided to remain seated on the bed, finishing his coffee, whilst listening to the sound of the water cascading down from the shower tap, picturing the warm jets of spray massaging her naked flesh and the jewels of water sparkling in the crevices of her lithe body.

He could hear Sandra singing as she bathed, obviously luxuriating in the warmth, although he could not quite place the song.

When he had drained the last of his coffee he glanced down into the empty cup, at the stain of brown liquid holding on to the edges of the china circle like limpets.

His mind had began to drift when Sandra appeared moments later, stepping back into the bedroom, hair wrapped in a towel, her lithe and sensuous body encased in white fluffy bath robe.

Droplets of water fell to the carpet to be absorbed by its thick pile.

Even now she still looked beautiful and Karl could honestly swear to not having seen a finer woman.

"Thank you for yesterday. I had a fantastic time."

"It was my pleasure." Sandra replied, smiling as she half closed her eyes in what was supposed to be a seductive manner, but in reality it looked like she was just short sighted, so needed to squint.

Karl had been an exquisite date and a fine lover so she hoped that this would not be the last time that she would ever see him.

Walking over to the bed, she removed the towel that had been twisted around the top of her head and began blotting her hair dry, noting that Karl was watching her every move, unable to tear his eyes away from her.

Enjoying the attention she slunk down onto the bed and lifted her arms.

"So... Do I not even get a good-morning kiss?"

Karl was only too happy to oblige as it was the invitation that he had been waiting for since she had awakened earlier.

As he reached over to touch her tender lips he felt the tears of self-pity begin to well in his eyes. Blinking them away he battled bravely as his body fought his mind, creating an inner riot of strange emotions, bottomless pits of lust fighting the urge to preserve her beauty in death.

Her long painted nails scratched down his back as he leant over her, propped up on his elbow.

Still battling his inner demons he breathed heavily, his nostrils savouring the scent from the tea tree shower cream that now emanated from her body. He just wished that the stain of guilt could as easily be cleansed from him...

Sandra was just so lovely, so utterly desirable that he felt bewitched, but his shadowed eyes held a dark secret, perhaps a secret destiny that would ultimately destroy them both.

Not sensing the inner battle currently taking place within him, Sandra wrapped her arms around his body pulling Karl down on top of her, her lips and tongue searching for his mouth, their bodies pressed firmly together.

She felt the rough stubble of his chin on hers, jolting an urge of desire that sprung up from between her legs.

Karl was now feeling equal desire but still juggling with his inner demons as no one could know the pain of betrayal until they had been betrayed. Shaking the thought from his mind he pressed his body down firmly, possessively almost, against hers.

She sensed his desires echoing hers as his breathing intensified and the arousal became visually apparent. His lust had temporarily won out over his fury, though his knuckles had turned white during the internal conflict, a visual display as to how hard the choice had actually been.

Karl began nibbling softly at Sandra lips, moving slowly to her ear lobe, his tongue flicking warmly like Gene Simmons in full flow, his breathing quickening all the while. His mind turned inwardly, eradicating the previous turmoil to concentrate on the pleasures of the flesh, whilst his body moving in time with hers, made tiny movements and prickles of excitement before the main event.

His hands moved over the surface of her silken body with a gentleness that belied his physique.

Sandra shuddered, throwing her head back into the plumped pillows as passion and ecstasy took hold. She closed her eyes, relishing the forthcoming act.

Karl's nuzzling lips had now moved from her ear lobe to her neck, where they nipped at her flesh like a swarm of hungry mosquitoes.

She shuddered deliciously, delighting in the mounting pleasure. She felt Karl's lightning rod twitch and spasm against the inside of her thigh, so she knew that his body had felt her response. She lay back, revelling in his dominance, thrusting against him as he pinned her arms above her head, exercising his control. His lips continued to press about her flesh, making tiny pecking movements, butterfly kisses, along her neck and cheek before moving southward to her now exposed and willing breasts.

She opened her eyes and followed his dark head, whilst her body tremored to the drum beat of sexual desire. Karl's tongue darted out like a viper, teasing her hardening nipples before he encased each of them in turn between his eager lips, sucking at them like teats from a baby's bottle.

"Mmmm", he whispered against her breast, as if in response to the murmurings of desire that she had been omitting. With his own urgency taking over, he sucked hard, drawing her swollen nipples into his mouth and between his fingers.

He then edged himself up to thrust his mouth against hers, and she felt as though she was drowning in him, as his tongue filled her mouth, stopping her words and breath in the same instant. Finally she remembered to breathe, as her body responded and dampness seeped against her inner thigh. Her tongue found his and they exchanged rapier like thrusts as if engaged in a dual. She proceeded to wrap her legs around his waist and drew him in to her. She gasped at the jolt and then moaned softly as he moved inside her, gradually reducing the speed of his thrusts to a more languid movement.

He continued to hold her wrists as he gyrated above her, his eyes piercing hers as she playfully fought against the restraint.

Unable to control the waves of orgasm erupting from his body, Karl groaned and pressed his head against her heaving breasts as he climaxed inside her.

Lust and pain came together as their bodies exchanged and shared the moment of orgasm.

Sandra leaned her head backwards onto the pillows, closing her eyes, radiating in the pleasure of the climax and the domination.

With his own urgency now sated, Karl began to kiss her again, although this time attempting to please her, rather than himself. He released her wrists, so that his hands could now caress her smooth and delicate skin, moulding them over her breasts as he suckled lightly, tenderly.

As he did so, her nails dug into the flesh of his back, lightly at first then a bit harder, like a lioness urging her mate to play.

Karl moaned gently as her fingers dug deeper into his soft flesh, now with undeniable urgency...

Taking charge she moved him to one side so that she could now sit astride him. Her eyes drilled into his as their bodies melted into pleasure, his swollen rod sliding relentlessly into her body like a piston, as she gyrated seductively above him.

His eyes glazed as he stretched and filled her pussy lips, his hands involuntarily flexing and relaxing with the pleasure that he was experiencing. Sandra was currently controlling his body and he was delighting in it...

Eventually her body lifted as they orgasmed together, both crying out in the bonding of pleasure.

For a while after there was a silence, as lust sated, they lay breathless together, entwined as if their bodies were melting candles.

Finally Sandra pecked at his chest and he slipped his erection out of her.

After Karl had disengaged himself from her, they lay a moment longer basking in the warm glow of orgasmic fulfilment as his fingers caressed her golden hair and swept across her cheek. A tiny smile played across his lips as the experience of the last twenty-four hours were as different from the previous darkness of his life as they could possibly be.

Unfortunately for Karl it would not be long before memories of long ago once again began to bubble to the surface and questions such as 'Why was he not given sanctuary as a child?' would be asked...

To this day he could still hear the voices of the social worker mingling with his mother's, talking and laughing as he sat crouched and hungry in his punishment cupboard, too afraid of the possible consequences to cry out for assistance but not willingly choosing to remain living with parents that beat him. Although the marks had long since faded he could still feel the cigarettes burning deep into his arms and legs and in his mind's eye he could almost see the welts rising once again...

He was sure that the results of this inner struggle would remain with him until he was just dust in the ground.

CHAPTER 12

THE PRESS CALL

Detective Inspector Ross pushed through the swinging door and into the police station's reception area, waiting to be buzzed through to the back.

Seated behind the reception desk was a tall thickset officer with dark but close cropped hair, who was attempting to combine the roles of gracious receptionist and security guard, although it was hard to imagine this no-necked, lank shouldered officer being able to perform anything remotely administrative. He looked as though mere speech would prove to be somewhat of a challenging task.

From what Detective Inspector Ross could ascertain the East European officer in question was currently attempting to deal with a complaint from an Asian shopkeeper regarding vandalism and shoplifting. As both parties were speaking in broken English, they appeared to be getting nowhere fast.

Detective Inspector Ross raised his eyes skyward in a gesture that spoke his unuttered thoughts.

Just where was this positive discrimination going to end?

The desk officer finally realizing that he was stood waiting to be buzzed through obliged before uttering a brief apology. He then returned his attention to the irate shopkeeper to resume their round of verbal fencing.

As echoes of Pidgin English floated up the stairwell, Detective Inspector Ross made his way up to his office.

He was feeling nervous as he had a press call followed by a meeting, with Detective Chief Inspector Andy Burns, later in the day, to discuss the case and the new unfurling developments within it.

He had dressed for the occasion, hoping to feign an air of confidence as to how the investigation was progressing. Hence, he was crisply attired in a tailored black blazer and trousers, complete with creases that he was sure could slice paper. The showy ensemble was completed by a freshly starched white shirt and a charcoal grey tie.

He felt uncomfortable in the clothes but just prayed that they would succeed in projecting the image and air of confidence that he wished to portray.

The spectre of failure already floated about him, so he could not afford for anything else to delay an arrest. He was determined to take advantage of the moment and obtain the prize that he sought the most. He just had to grab a few handwritten notes off his desk and once again go through his intended speech before addressing the waiting media throng that would he suspected soon be gathering outside.

He took slow regular breaths in a bid to remain calm and to keep his senses together.

During the night, the police incident room had received an avalanche of calls – a high majority claiming that a man matching the description of the published Photofit had been seen in or about the same local area.

A Meadowbank Drive had been mentioned by many of the callers.

A variety of names had also been put forward – all of whom would now need to be methodically tracked down and eliminated from the enquiry.

As a result of the flood of calls, local housing and criminal records were once again being re-examined for that area and cross matched with any of the new names put forward from the carpet and hunting knife retailers and manufacturers.

It was likely to be a long and wearing process but hopefully one that would ultimately pay huge dividends. He just had to hope that the sweet milk of anticipation did not now begin to curdle.

Feeling apprehension again begin to take hold, he fished out a cigarette from the pack within his jacket pocket. As he lit the cancer stick and inhaled, breathing a deep lungful, he promised himself that it would definitely be the last one to ever touch his lips. For now, he needed its false assurance in order to maintain his well rehearsed pleasant and self confident manner – a requisite of senior ranking officers.

He grabbed the case and speech notes from off of his desk, ignoring the incessant chirping pleas of the telephone to lift its receiver.

Whatever and whoever it was could wait. He had to collect his thoughts and remember his lines, so he did not want to deal with anything else on top of that just at the moment.

The telephone, as though sensing defeat, reluctantly ceased its ringing.

He then found that the silence made him feel ever more nervous and on edge than the incessant trilling tone had done. As part of his brain contemplated whether he would have time for another cigarette before the press call, the remainder was still frantically memorizing the speech.

Much like with an Academy award winner, he had to make sure that his words did not upset anyone or would later come back to bite him on the arse…

CHAPTER 13

INNER TURMOIL

Karl managed to hail a taxicab to get back home. He stared idly out of the car window as the driver droned on about sport, politics and quite often nothing in particular.

Karl took delight in viewing the parts of London that the journey home represented as it stopped him from building up a basic frustration at the recent build up of traffic.

Cars at present were bumper to bumper and moving at the pace of an arthritic snail.

As the cab driver droned on, seemingly oblivious to the fact that his musings on life, the universe and everything were receiving no response from Karl aside from the odd grunt of acknowledgement, Karl began to silently ask himself the question: 'Why couldn't the traffic be okay, just this once?!'

He now wanted to get home before his frustration and anxiety manifested so that his head would not be filled with dark and ugly thoughts.

He began to wonder if it may not be quicker for him to walk…

Thankfully moments later the traffic began to move at a more regular speed and his spirits rose disproportionately at this tiny change of fortune.

To others it would probably seem odd that being prevented from getting where he wanted to go had caused such anxiousness but Karl did not enjoy the sensation of his destiny not being within his own hands or on this occasion the inane ramblings of a taxi-cab driver whose political views appeared to be slightly to the right of Ghenghis Khan...

Although in reality the taxi journey home from Sandra's was relatively painless Karl still felt ill at ease, his mind a conundrum comprising pieces that just did not seem to fit together. Various fragments of the previous night's imaginings had been swimming around his head since he had got up, but none of these would resonate. All were ephemeral – just bits and pieces that swam around his head for a short period before he had awoken properly.

There was a brief pause, during which he felt the impact of recent memory, like hazy nostalgia experienced all too soon; electric though the encounter with Sandra had been, he feared that the passion of their first night together may never be topped. Karl's heart sank a little for his indecision was causing a spiritual hardship.

He felt a terrible guilt that turned at intervals into a raging anger at the world, which was interspersed with feelings of love for Sandra. The combination of the three very different emotions seemed to be taking him and twisting him violently up and around like litter caught in the middle of a hurricane.

He could sense himself playing some kind of active role in the dynamic but that did not help the feeling that his passions were caught up in an endless spiral of confusion and uncertainty...

Perhaps he just needed a break to clear his head and plan things out?

He was considering asking Sandra to join him but it seemed too soon for such a step – after all, love was a very new sensation for him.

A weekend away seemed to be an interim answer and definitely more enjoyable than the prospect of his immediate future. His life would be held in suspension until he had come to a decision…perfect.

He pictured himself driving down to the Kent coastline on Friday to breathe in the salty air and to laze upon the golden sands before driving back on the Sunday.

His mind was made up…

Karl finally reached his abode, the taxicab screeching to an abrupt halt at the kerbside.

Karl slid a ten pound note into the driver's palm and promptly alighted from the car.

He stood momentarily ensconced upon the pavement as the taxi driver revved the vehicle's engine.

As Karl's shoes crunched over his graveled driveway he heard the taxicab pull away into the oncoming traffic, causing the driver behind to honk his car horn furiously, the sound akin to a distressed goose.

Karl slipped the house key into the lock on the front door and twisted it to enter his premises.

He closed the door behind him and walking into the living room he settled himself down on the settee before clicking the Technics compact disc player to life.

The strains of Guns and Roses filtered from the speakers.

Karl reached down to the remote control and turned the volume up a few notches. 'Welcome to the jungle' was always a song that had moved him and he wanted to listen to it as loudly as possible, to have his soul swamped by it…

Several tracks later Karl stirred out of the trance of music and walked towards the living room window to ease it open. He stood framed at the window, staring out onto the street below as the breeze blew wisps of his fringe across his eyes.

Axl Rose was still singing loudly, spitting venom at the world for all its cruelties and injustices.

Karl mouthed the words in sync delighting in the momentary loss of self and worry.

Fifty-three minutes and fifty-one seconds later Axl's caterwauling ceased leaving Karl to retreat back onto the sofa.

Sitting down on the settee, Karl's mind went into a mental vacuity, a dead time, as he reached over to the drinks cabinet and poured himself a large tumbler of Jack Daniels bourbon whisky.

He drank the generous measure quickly as if he were playing a cowboy who had just picked up the glass from the slide along bar. The strength and warmth of the liquor momentarily stunned his tongue and throat, leaving his breath rasping. He refilled the tumbler but intended to savour the taste of the whisky this time.

Something had been bugging him all morning, something that had been lying in wait within his consciousness – a feeling similar to the realization that he had forgotten something. With that feeling he was attempting to back-date the sensation – the feeling of his brain nagging at itself. But, it was of no use – the time before the dreamlike memory would not come to his beckoning. The images that did, however, made him shiver so much that he chased them; he chased them away in his head…

Karl dropped his shoulders and breathed in deeply in an attempt to further aid his quest for relaxation. Grabbing the remote control to the compact disc player off of the arm of the settee he moved the volume back down to its original level and then pressed the play button to kick-start the next disc.

The mood suddenly mellowed as the sultry husky tones of Stevie Nicks filled the room, her velveteen voice complementing the serenity that he was now beginning to feel. His feet began tapping gently in time with the bass lines whilst, in between swigs of Jack Daniels, his lips moved silently to the lyrics. He listened appreciatively as the warmth in Stevie Nicks' voice made him feel as though he were wrapped in the wings of a guardian angel.

He felt weary but self-satisfied and for a brief moment all was right with the world…

1am

Clad in only his towelling robe Karl wandered barefoot through his deserted home, nursing his ritual remedy for insomnia – an extremely large measure of Des Ribauds "Hommage Au Temps" 50-year-old Cognac. Karl put the brandy to his mouth. The tumbler covered his mouth too and for a while he left it there, attempting to lose himself in the overpowering scent of the alcohol. Then he drank it all down in one go. Reaching down for the decanter he filled up his glass, an even larger measure this time.

The moon filtered through the bay window and illuminated the intense hues of the plush carpeting and reflected off the bookshelves which were packed with books (as he was an avid reader of a variety of genres).

He flicked on the light switch and walked over to the shelves where he selected the latest novel from the pen of Stephen King. The lighting angled a wash of shadows across the room making everything look drawn and stretched. He took a seat in his favourite armchair before settling down to savour the warmth of the Cognac.

Karl caught his reflection in the glass, a seemingly haunted image – distorted and pale. He felt old. His youthful spirit had been crushed at an early age and now he was just residing in a mortal shell, his soul long since vacated.

It was as though he could not exist without carrying excess baggage. His mind trawling the mists of time, back to when he was a small child constantly dressed in thick woolly jumpers and long trousers to hide the bruises and scars. It was a shame that the mental ones were taking longer to heal as his previous self-confidence was bleeding from a thousand unseen wounds. He would often lie awake in bed, unable to sleep, speaking out loud as if trying to push out the disturbing memories from his mind. He realized that such things needed to be expelled but was unsure as to how that very goal may be ultimately achieved. He felt withdrawn, a tense ball of fear and loneliness. He yearned for his head to be blank of thoughts and dreams but alas his night was being sandblasted with insomnia, a frantic sleeplessness.

Karl moved his hand away from the glass and picked at the cushion until its seam was as frazzled as his nerves. His thoughts turned to Sandra attempting to renew the memory of their first night together. He had always avoided commitment in the past and the thought that he would ever meet someone with whom he would form a connexion had never even really stayed within his consciousness for more than a fleeting moment in time. Sandra was obviously attractive but she also had an air of dignified intelligence and seemed so in-tune with his own needs and instincts. The onrush of these new feelings tumbled over one another as they entered his heart.

Promises were dangerous.

He shivered slightly, his mirrored image rippling slightly like the surface of still water. Their second date was imminent but until then the mental imagery would have to suffice…

As he dipped his head down to peruse the novel, wisps of his thick chestnut brown hair toppled forward onto his forehead, temporarily masking his crinkled brow.

After reading less than a dozen pages, he gave up admitting defeat. He just could not seem to focus his mind as a battle was currently raging within him.

He felt tense, his senses flooded. Despite the febrile nature of his murderous urges and impulses, he felt shame, but embroiled within it were excitement, lust, stimulation and fear. But it was shame nonetheless.

Half of him yearned to embrace his new found optimism and partner, the other half wary of building up hope or dependence on anyone. He knew better than most that everyone was out for number one and that the law of the jungle had always applied. If you did not trust or depend on anyone you could never be disappointed.

Karl took another sip of his drink, felt the brandy go into his mouth and at the same time he felt his gullet start to tremble. He let his cheeks fill with the Cognac and looked down to the plush carpeted floor.

Raising his eyes, he stared across at his home computer terminal, which sat perched upon his broad oak desk like an ancient monolith, but could not muster enough interest to even log on. It was a sure sign that he was getting old as he now bypassed the bombardment of pornographic sites and only used the internet for banking or international news.

As Karl sat alone he absently gazed into the semi darkness of the world outside his window, whilst drinking in the silence and serenity of his home.

That emotional comfort was short lived as his mind began tugging him in a direction that he did not want to go but he felt too exhausted to be annoyed.

He stifled a yawn. Wearily he levered himself out of the armchair and returned his empty brandy glass to the kitchen before walking slowly to his bedroom.

It was late, well past midnight, the night perfectly silent as Karl lapsed back into sleep, his mind churning over a mixture of emotions – regret, sorrow, but also anger and resentment; a labyrinth of dreams within his fractured mind…

He stirred under the duvet as his mind lowered him into the dark, lulling him into a deeper slumber, tricking him into opening the portal to the ghosts and the buried memories that forever stalked his existence.

A fearful look clouded his sleeping face, as if eager to enact his mind's fantasies upon his features. As rage gnashed within him, his dreams became overwhelmed by a feeling that he had stretched his luck too far. He could almost hear the time bomb ticking away, leaving him in a meaningless void…

CHAPTER 14

THE BREAKTHROUGH

The murder squad had spent the last few hours gathering the facts, each person on the team adding what he or she knew to the puzzle. Now they were just trying to piece it all together to form some coherent whole.

The thrill of any previous successes was now just a distant echo as they sought to match and cross-match the data that they had.

Meanwhile, on the floor above, Detective Inspector Ross was currently in the process of briefing Detective Chief Inspector Burns on the developments, minimal as they were, thus far.

Detective Inspector Ross was wearing clothes that, although quite smart, were currently lying untidily upon him; he looked very tired in the face, and a little ill. His eyes were encircled by dark rings, which made him look like a giant panda, and bags the size of suitcases, which were obviously a more than vivid testimony as to recent insomnia and how much the enquiry was taking out of him.

Detective Inspector Ross paused to take a much needed sip of coffee before continuing with the fresh flow of words. He spoke slowly, steadily, in a measured tone, as he knew that he could not risk losing his composure in front of a superior officer.

"I realize that you have the Commissioner breathing down your neck, but this is our top priority. Everyone is looking for him. We have made television appeals; the newspapers (both local and national) have all printed his likeness, and his description has been circulated to every officer within the Metropolitan area. We have already had many reported sightings, pleasingly a large section within the same few streets. We will continue to do everything we possibly can do, including house to house enquiries, to find him; I can firmly assure you of that."

Just as Detective Chief Inspector Burns was about to respond, his telephone chirped to life. He grunted a response as he raised the receiver (which felt like ivory) up to his ear.

His throat crackled, sounding dry but as Detective Inspector Ross's eyes travelled over him he noted his lips curling upwards into the barest of smiles.

At this action Detective Inspector Ross instantly became consumed with curiousity, his ears on stalks for the hints of enlightenment that were slow in coming.

As Detective Inspector Ross looked on in puzzled silence, Detective Chief Inspector Burns quickly scribbled on the notepad in front of him as he listened intently to the information that the caller was imparting to him.

After a seemingly lengthy pause, he tore off part of the page on which he had been scribbling and held it out in view of the Inspector.

Detective Inspector Ross glanced down at the sheet of scrap paper that was being shown to him. On it was an underlined name that was unfamiliar to him. He assumed from Detective Chief Inspector Burn's expression that whatever news he was now receiving it was good, but failed to see what connection this Karl Connor had with it. Nevertheless, his attention had been grabbed and now he was aching to know the details of the seemingly one-way telephone conversation. He stood transfixed, focused on the telephone, eagerly awaiting the receiver to go down and the new information to be imparted to him.

Detective Chief Inspector Burns' tone had softened and eventually he terminated the call, with the note of gratitude echoing deep within his voice.

"This is it. We have got the guy. This Karl Connor appears on invoice records for the items we were looking for and also census reports confirm that he lives in the road where the previous sightings were given – not long moved in apparently, so it looks like we have finally nailed the bastard."

Detective Inspector Ross, raising an eyebrow, was momentarily taken aback, his mind whirling with the news and the realization that after almost a year-long struggle a satisfactory conclusion was now in sight. He felt like a man awakening from a long sleep.

Now came all the logistics of organizing the raid and search operation. An arrest warrant would need to be sanctioned and a search warrant would need to be obtained for the property and any other properties owned by the suspect in question. Then a time and date plan would need to be formulated and one 'person-in-charge' selected prior to the arrival at the scene. The necessary safety considerations of the search personnel would also need to be met and satisfied, hence an armed response unit would be on hand as they approached, secured and protected the scene.

Detective Inspector Ross realized that he would also have to organize a command post headquarters for communication, decision making etc, as on no account could they afford this operation to go pear-shaped. As soon as he himself was made aware of all the facts, he would need to discuss the upcoming search with his murder squad personnel and organize communication with services of an ancillary nature, in order that any questions or problems that surfaced during the crime scene search may be resolved there and then. His thoughts were now positively reeling with the prospect of conducting the final act of this massive police operation.

Detective Chief Inspector Andy Burns' voice suddenly snapped him from his rapidly spiralling train of thought and he listened intently to the developments thus far.

The Driver and Vehicle Licensing Agency (DVLA) at Swansea had been contacted, so they now knew the make, model, colour and registration number of the car that Karl Connor drove. An all points bulletin on both the suspect and the car would soon be issued, as time was of the essence. In addition, seaports and airports would be notified, should he decide to flee the country.

If Karl killed again before they had the opportunity to detain him they would all be kissing goodbye to their healthy Civil Service pensions.

They now knew the killer's identity and the wave of relief that had washed over the both of them was plainly evident.

The pain and trauma of the last year was at last beginning to fade, as for now they were both engulfed in a wave of renewed optimism. They put aside the nagging doubt that it may not be too easy to obtain a search warrant as the evidence was thin and circumstantial but hopefully the media coverage and the emotional impact of the cases would force even the hardest nosed judge to sway any decision in their favour.

Detective Inspector Ross plotted the process in his mind.

"How many people live in the target's house?"

Detective Chief Inspector Burns' eyes glanced downward to double-check his scribbled notes before responding.

"Just him, we think. He is listed as the sole occupant but obviously we will have the premises under surveillance to double-check this, before we move in. Obviously once we have initiated the preliminary survey and determined the boundaries, we can cut off any possible escape routes and organize the method and procedure for taking him down."

"It will be nice to finally put this one to bed as it has been eating away at me like a cancer."

A heavy silence then fell between them until it was shattered by the sound of Detective Chief Inspector Burns' office telephone sparking to life, issuing insistent trills, and urging his attention.

Before picking up the receiver he excused Detective Inspector Ross, who eager to get the ball rolling, headed straight down to the murder squad's incident room to debrief his team and get the wheels in motion regarding the pending search warrant.

CHAPTER 15

ASSIGNATION

After running himself a bath, Karl lay in the water until his body felt relaxed; his mind, though, was deep in thought. The all too familiar inner voice inside his head was tugging at his emotions, now urging him to kill again; a tiny memory – like a trace.

His brows involuntarily arched, before he squeezed his eyes shut, the bathroom diminishing into darkness to be replaced by memories, glimpses from a seemingly unforgotten past. He knew deep down that things did not change, they just looked different, rearranged, as his heart had betrayed him and fate had pinned him like a moth to a card, the road to sanctity as elusive as ever.

As he lay submerged beneath the lapping ripples, he murmured to himself, his thoughts and dreams enjoying a voice of their own, a haunted whisper that curled chillingly in his listening ears. He feared that he might be losing his mind, his own perception being called into question.

Usually he found that a long soak in a hot bubble bath infused with the scent of vanilla and mimosa was relaxing. He enjoyed steeping in the warm water and topping it up at regular intervals, but today was different as although his body was luxuriating in the pampering of the essential bath oils, his mind, deep in thought, was spinning like a hamster on a wheel, never relenting. The prospect of a net curtain twitching future was now at the forefront of his mind.

Eventually giving up on the goal of unwinding he stepped out of the bathtub and yanked the plug free from its resting place. As the water trickled away, gurgling like a contented infant, he quickly towelled himself dry and opening the bathroom door, padded through to his bedroom.

He flung open the wardrobe door and lifted a pair of black pleated trousers down from their hanger. He then grabbed a white shirt, clean socks and boxer shorts from their respective drawers.

He was meeting Sandra later, so needed to look his dapper best. Once attired to his satisfaction he walked softly through to the kitchen in order to prepare a quick drink and a bite to eat.

Whilst the coffee percolator bubbled effervescently Karl reheated the remainder of the previous night's take away curry.

Minutes later he was sat in front of the television, tray on lap, with the chicken tikka masala about to sate his current pangs of hunger.

He took a sip of coffee, followed by a mouthful of curry, the tastes combining into a warm, spicy flavour that prickled his tongue and warmed his throat.

He pinched his eyes between thumb and forefinger before forcing them back open.

Reaching across to pick up the remote control off the arm of the settee he clicked the television set to life before channel hopping in a vain bid to find a news item or at the very least something slightly intellectual. Alas, the height of daytime stimulus appeared to consist of menopausal women discussing the most inane topics. He had not encountered the programme 'Loose Women' before today, but by the look of them 'loose' was being kind as they all looked as though they were positively falling apart.

Reaching for the remote control he clicked the television set to the standby mode and finished the rest of his meal in peace.

After the previous moment of banality, he could not help but to agree that in this instance silence was indeed golden.

With his stomach now fully sated he stood up and walking into the kitchen, deposited the tray and crockery into the double sink.

He would wash them up later, as for now he had more pressing engagements.

He began to walk out of the room, but he stopped to momentarily glance out of the front window – it looked to be a beautifully clear day, without a cloud in the sky.

He strolled over to the bathroom to clean his teeth and to run a brush through his hair. Eyeing himself in the shaving mirror positioned on the small shelf above the sink he looked and felt ready to face the world.

As he vacated his house he pulled up the collar to his jacket and fastened the buttons, as a sudden wind whipped through his clothes, cutting through the thin shirt that he was attired in.

The temperature felt a lot cooler than of late, but aside from the wind tossed hair, the slight discomfort was not so bad.

His gaze fell upon his beloved silver-grey metallic BMW M3 convertible, now reflecting that perhaps due to all the media attention he would have to downgrade to a much less conspicuous car.

He got into the vehicle and slid the keys into the ignition as he pulled the car door shut.

His thoughts exhilarating but ominous, as he put the car into gear and began to reverse slowly out of the driveway, the gravel crackling like firecrackers beneath the weight of the tyres.

He edged slowly out, seeking a space in the traffic in which to slip neatly into.

As he pulled out, the breeze brought the scent of roses floating to his nostrils, the same fragrance that he remembered from his mother's garden all those years ago.

His mind drifted, mulling over the decades to the domain that he had now created. His previous calm was now once again beginning to crumble as he was now troubled. An all too familiar image was invading his finely tuned world.

The breeze that filtered through the partially open car window tugged at his hair and clothes, billowing them gently away from his body. The sudden draught snapped his mind away from his darkening thoughts, diverting them back onto his assignation with Sandra.

This prospect brought to mind other, more immediate delights that hopefully would lay in store for him tonight.

He felt the beginnings of an erection begin to stir within his boxer shorts, but being temporarily kept at bay by its encasement. He felt happy when he was with her, uplifted by her presence or even just the thought of her. He had a flash vision of Sandra naked and he inhaled deeply hoping to calm himself down before he arrived at his destination.

Minutes later his car glided to a halt in the customer's car park to the rear of the St. Georges Tavern.

Glancing at his watch he realized that he was a tad early, but he decided to wait inside.

Gazing up at the structure he could not help but to feel that this historic public house looked quite surreal given the built up area in which it was located. It looked as though someone had dropped it there from some discarded movie set. It was a large mediaeval-looking building, impressively grandiose, and probably the only building of any architectural note within the whole borough.

Although not a royalist by any stretch of the imagination he could not help but to agree with Prince Charles when he likened modern architecture to unsightly carbuncles. The giant Tesco store opposite the St Georges Tavern was a case in point, a huge glass structure that looked like a giant greenhouse, with fittings and fixtures that looked like they had been designed by a visually impaired yuppie whilst on some surreal acid trip.

Aside from his own car, the tavern's gravel parking lot currently hosted three other cars, a couple of 4x4 off road vehicles (for some reason a necessity for London roads and school runs by mothers with more children than brain cells) and a sorry looking teal Ford Mondeo, which had obviously known better days. On closer inspection both the wing mirrors, paintwork and the front and rear bumpers had suffered damage, so either the driver was just very unlucky or had driven it around like a fairground dodgem car.

Karl clicked into operation the alarm on his own car and made his way to the Tavern's entrance, eager to peruse the lunchtime menu and enquire about the specials, before Sandra arrived.

He knew from experience that a little knowledge could go a long way.

He reached the large oak door and swung it open pausing momentarily before deciding to enter.

Inside he found that the establishment was brightly lit and elegantly decorated. An original antique fireplace took centre stage, and although currently unlit it made for a dramatic conversation piece. The overall result was that a peaceful, calming and almost homely feel had been successfully achieved.

Glancing to his right, into the restaurant area, he saw shadowy figures hunched over their dinner plates, seemingly deep in conversation.

Karl approached the bar, whereupon the bartender, whose olive skin and raven hair was accentuated by his pristine white shirt, ceased wiping down the counter to take his drink order.

As Karl looked around he noted that the heavily beamed walls of the Tavern were clotted with posters and framed black and white photos depicting the area in a bygone era. He could not help but to note how much the location had changed, and not for the better...

The barman of indeterminate race returned with Karl's red wine, before he went back to wiping down the counter, his cloth gently sweeping over the glowing neon signs that were promoting a variety of over priced and under strength lagers from around the four corners of the globe.

Karl ran his fingers through his hair and slowly removed his hand from his crown, feeling the hairs fall forward like tumbling dominoes freed from their pulled taut line.

As Karl sat waiting at the bar, sipping on his drink, echoes of conversation drifted through from the dining area, where suit clad businessmen were dining and swapping loud and unbelievable stories.

Karl had always been a great believer in the statement, 'Those who can, do. Those who can't, talk'.

Karl pulled up a bar stool and took a sip of wine, delighting in its rich texture and bouquet, a delightful scent of red berry fruit.

The comforting smell of freshly cooked food filtered through from the restaurant area, tantalizing his eager taste buds still further.

As he glanced around looking for the menus, he felt a slight draught prickle his skin as the tavern's main door opened inwards.

Sandra entered and he waved good-naturedly at her, in acknowledgment.

She returned his actions with a beaming smile and outstretched arms, ready for an embrace, as she approached him. She looked positively stunning and radiant, even though she was casually but elegantly 'dressed down' in a white Donna Karen cotton tee shirt, short lacy white summer skirt and delicately strapped open toed shoes.

Karl was not sure if she was aware but her nipples were clearly visible through the skimpy top, attracting his attention and probably the notice of several of the other male customers.

Sandra kissed him, her lips spreading like margarine upon his. He kissed her back tenderly at first then more passionately, welcoming the pleasure that had encased him.

As their lips parted he battled to keep the smile out of his voice.

"What would you like to drink?"

"What are you drinking?"

"A Californian Merlot."

"That sounds nice, I will have the same."

As Sandra looked Karl up and down, she smiled internally as well.

Karl attracted the bartender's attention and waited for the order to be processed and the drink totals added to his tab, before returning his full attention to Sandra before speaking again.

"You look absolutely stunning."

"Thank you. So do you. I hope that you haven't been waiting long."

"Gosh, no, not at all. I arrived just a few minutes before you. I was just admiring the furnishings. It's a nice place, first time that I have seen it from the inside, and it seems very cosy."

"Yes, I like it."

Feeling that they were regrettably still in the margin of small talk Sandra exhaled, puffing her lips out, pouting, as she did so.

As she eyed Karl again her eyes narrowed a little and a tingle of pure lust shuddered through her body.

Karl looked gorgeous and she was sorely tempted to just entice him into one of the establishment's scattered alcoves, to see how far they could get before they were discovered. She dismissed the tantalizing thought from her mind and tried to focus on more constructive ideas.

Sandra raised the long stemmed wine glass to her lips in a bid to bide time and regain some of her inner composure.

The next few hours or so, saw them discuss life, the universe and seemingly every topic imaginable, whilst enjoying a closeness of people who had known each other a lifetime.

Relishing his gaze, Sandra watched Karl's eyes rake her body, his smile widening as if answering the ripples that were still cascading deep inside her.

"Would you like to eat now?"

With an effort Sandra brought her thoughts back to the matter in hand.

"Um, y-yes, that would be great. Thank you."

She looked at him smiling fondly but for a brief moment she thought that she saw some sadness in his eyes and couldn't imagine why; surely things were going well?

The question remained unanswered as she dismissed the thought from her mind – blaming it on her own paranoia.

Stepping down from their respective bar stools they made their way into the restaurant section. The earlier business lunch had ended, so only one other couple remained. They were currently being served desserts by a young waitress whose long golden locks were being kept at bay by a black velvet ribbon.

As the waitress approached them, she flashed a smile at Karl, before turning her gaze towards Sandra.

She handed them each a menu.

"Would you like a drink whilst you peruse the menus?"

Karl quickly eyed the wine list before answering.

"A bottle of Etude Carneros Pinot Noir, please."

"Very good, sir."

As the waitress exited to the wine cellar, Sandra leaned forward to study the menu, still unaware that her traitorous nipples continued to betray her sexual desire. She squashed the impulse and cast her eyes over the choices on offer, her brain momentarily flustered by the conflicting message that it was receiving. She studied the menu for a moment longer as the waitress approached them with their table wine and glasses.

The bottle of wine and two crystal long stemmed wine glasses were laid upon the tablecloth. Uncorking the wine, the waitress delicately poured a little of the rich red vino into each glass, awaiting their verdict.

Karl picked up his wine and swilled the blood red liquid gently around the glass, before sipping its contents.

"That's lovely thank you."

Sandra nodded silently in agreement.

"Are you ready to order now?"

It was Sandra who responded first, her taste buds now positively tingling in anticipation of the delights to come.

"May I have the soup of the day for starter and the Lamb Anatolian Style with courgettes, carrots and shallot onions for the main course? Thank you."

"And for you sir?"

"May I have the Mediterranean Prawns with Garlic for starter and the breast of chicken served with oyster mushroom and calvados sauce for the main course?"

"Very good, sir."

The waitress tucked her notebook into her waistcoat pocket and gathered up the menus, her fingers gently brushing Karl's palm as she did so. As she departed, Karl pretended not to have noticed, Sandra painted on a smile but was about to rise to the challenge.

Like a wildcat marking her territory, Sandra leaned back and pushed her chair gently away from the table. Her tee shirt rose slightly to expose her pierced navel and her nipples sprang to attention, relishing Karl's appreciative gaze.

Casually crossing her legs, she let the hem of her skirt ride up further to expose an expanse of trim, sleek-muscled thigh. Electric charges were currently being sent across the surface of the skin. She felt sexy just sitting there, flaunting her sexuality, showing off her body to Karl, whilst they made small talk.

The conversation came to an abrupt halt as the waitress approached them, tray in hand.

With mission accomplished, Sandra edged her chair back in towards the table, taking care not to unsettle the glasses of wine.

The waitress was balancing the two starters upon the same tray whilst attempting not to catch her heels on the restaurant carpet.

Sandra inwardly smiled, as obviously the waitress had chosen fashion over practicality and now resembled some tottering third-rate acrobat.

"Help yourselves to bread," invited the waitress as she approached the table, indicating to a basket of freshly baked mini rolls.

As the starters were laid in front of each of them in turn, both looked suitably impressed. Sandra realized that she was ravenous and helped herself to a couple of the rolls, breaking them up into her soup as if she were feeding ducks in the local mere.

They passed a pleasant quarter of an hour engaged in flirtatious chatter, as the starters were devoured with relish.

The bowls were cleared away before the main courses arrived, their aromatic scents flavouring the air, tempting their taste buds still further.

"Would you like a top up?"

Without waiting for a response, Karl poured a healthy measure of the rich red wine into her glass.

She smiled a 'thank you' as she slid off her shoe to glide her stockinged foot up and down Karl's calf.

As they tucked into the feast set before them, Sandra ached to tell Karl the truth about her profession, but something was holding her back though…perhaps a fear of losing him? He seemed respectable and upstanding enough, but she knew from bitter experience that men and her career was a match made in hell. Some felt resentful of the long shifts that she was forced to work, some the fact that she was surrounded all day by men and others just because they believed it was no job for a woman or simply because they could not abide the police force and what it now stood for. Sadly now, in many people's eyes, too many bad apples had soured the whole barrel. She had some sympathy for that mindset as she herself had experienced the dregs of the police force – racists, bigots, fascists, homophobes, male chauvinists, cheats and philanderers…and that was just the top brass.

As much as on the whole she enjoyed the job, she did also spend a fair percentage of her time wondering why she put up with certain aspects of it and whether her obvious people skills may be better served in a different and perhaps more rewarding occupation.

She obviously would tell Karl the truth about her career choice at some point soon (as she was very keen on him to say the least), but not just yet.

Sandra sucked in the air through her teeth as she cast her eyes around the restaurant. It was now empty. Around the bar sat a group of men, all attired in suits, with hairlines visibly receding at a rate of knots. She had always felt that 'male pattern baldness' was obviously the gods' way of ensuring that the mullet hairstyle never again made an appearance.

Feeling too full for dessert, she swallowed the last drop of wine and pushing the dinner plate away from her, excused herself to the ladies room, which was situated off to the rear of the bar.

She tried to walk nonchalantly but knew that Karl's eyes were upon her and she revelled in the continued flaunting of her sexuality. Hesitating outside the door to the ladies room, she heard soft footsteps falling in behind her. She turned to see Karl standing a few feet away. He stared at her, lust burning in his eyes, but his lips remaining silent. Sandra slowly pulled her tee-shirt clear from the waistband of her skirt and with pulse racing she deliberately allowed Karl another glimpse of her navel adornment. She backed towards the door to the ladies restroom and tested the elongated handle. It moved freely and so she slipped inside, holding it momentarily open in an act of silent invitation. Within moments Karl was with her, his hands closing the lock with a sharp snap. Inside the enclosed cubicle Karl grabbed at her body whilst she fumbled to get his shirt buttons undone. As her hands glided over his taut physique she felt his hands slide up beneath her tee shirt and gently cup her breasts. His fingers found her aching nipples and she stiffened as a jolt of pleasure shuddered through her body. Karl's torso was nearly hairless so her hands sculptured themselves over his well defined muscles. She quickly moved to unbuckle his belt before sliding his trousers and red and black Thai silk boxer shorts to the floor. His lightning rod had already sprung to life, curving upward towards his finely toned stomach like a cutlass unsheathed for action. Sandra caressed its shaft and pumped it playfully, enjoying the throbbing sensation in her hand. Her fingers reached down to cup his testicles. Karl groaned with pleasure and moved forward to kiss her. Instead of meeting his lips, she turned her head sideways, inviting his teeth to sink lightly into her neck. Still holding Karl's rod, Sandra backed up to the toilet and perched on the low cistern. The white porcelain was cold but the momentary chill was bearable in the circumstances. Releasing his pulsating rod, she spread her legs and lifted her skirt.

Without further invitation Karl straddled the closed toilet seat and plunged his rapier-like tongue into Sandra's heavenly shaven sex lips. She quivered in pleasure at his touch and purred with desire as his tongue buried deep within her.

Sandra caressed his hair, sliding her long slender fingers through his thick brunet locks before playfully grabbing them to push his face tighter into her groin. She buckled her hips to increase the pressure and friction. She orgasmed moments later, a swift delicious current that rippled from her pulsing bud through her body to reach her fingers and toes. Before the ripples had subsided Sandra slid down onto the toilet seat and presented her wide-open lips to Karl. She hooked her legs over his shoulders and drew him towards her, guiding his rod inside her with one fluid and experienced motion. Leaning back, Sandra used all the power in her toned thighs to hold Karl captive, unmoving, whilst his throbbing rod filled her.

Releasing him slightly, Sandra allowed Karl to thrust himself a little way in and out, gradually relaxing her hold until his firm rod was ramming into her like a piston. She slipped her fingers around her little bud, pleasuring herself in time to Karl's increasingly rapid thrusts. She sensed Karl's approaching climax and felt his warmth spill within her. She relaxed into him, her body moulding like liquid against his.

They sat breathless for a moment before kissing passionately, their lips hungry and still eager for each other. They were interrupted by the sound of the outer toilet door opening and someone entering an adjacent cubicle.

Karl said nothing but raised an inquisitive eyebrow before playfully biting down on Sandra's lip to curtail her giggling.

Time seemed to stand still as both of them held their breath, awaiting the other person to exit.

Each stifling their giggles, Sandra stood up and straightened her tee shirt before hitching down her skirt. She watched as Karl pulled up his boxer shorts and trousers, before fastening his shirt buttons and tucking his shirt into his waistband.

They stood silent as they heard the sound of the chain being pulled and the adjacent cubicle door clicking open. The sound of running water followed to be succeeded by a long and seemingly endless blast from an air hand dryer.

Minutes later the noise culminated in the outer toilet door being opened before clicking resoundingly shut.

Sandra slipped out of the cubicle and scanned the room. It was empty.

She quickly checked her appearance in the mirror before walking to the door. Opening it slightly she peered through. The bar was still relatively empty, so no eyes were currently focused in her direction.

Turning, she beckoned to Karl that the coast was clear and he exited the cubicle. He gave a dry laugh before he followed her from the ladies powder room, head bowed, eyes to the floor, as if he were a naughty schoolboy.

As they walked through the main room of the bar, the buzz of conversation died to be replaced by a series of nudges. They felt the eyes of the men, who were seated at the bar, upon them.

Damn, rumbled…

Karl felt instantly abashed whilst Sandra lowered her head.

She felt her cheeks flush as her face reddened, although inwardly she was still laughing at her impulsive behaviour.

"Let's just pay and get out of here," she whispered to Karl, her tone remaining gently buoyant.

"I have already taken care of the bill, just head for the exit!"

They strode out of the main door without looking left or right, both trying to hold in the mixture of laughter and embarrassment that were currently bubbling away in equal measures inside them.

Karl gave Sandra an affectionate look as they exited into the evening shadows of the narrow car park and headed towards his car. For a second Sandra had reservations about getting into a car with someone who had been drinking but chose not to voice her concerns once she found out that Karl lived less than ten minutes drive away.

Besides his car was just too expensive to leave in a pub car park overnight, come tomorrow chances were that it would have either vanished or be found burnt out and perched on bricks.

As they climbed into the car Sandra was slowly coming back to reality. She could not believe what she had just done and was shocked by her own lewd behaviour. Subconsciously she was clocking up the number of misdemeanors she had now committed. Her mind though, bored with her renewed conservatism, decided to replay the newly erotic memories and images as a faint tingle emanated from her little bud, reviving the sensations she had felt just a few minutes earlier.

Her body and mind both equally delighted that she had the following day off work as well...

A short while later, with everything back under control, she found herself within Karl's kitchen pouring out two hefty portions of Chateau La Raze Beauvallet into their respective glasses. Sandra angled her face towards Karl's but was silent for a moment as she sipped at the obligatory glass of red wine appreciatively.

She set her glass down on the glass coffee table, before throwing her arms around Karl and hugging him tightly, kissing him on the lips whilst playfully ruffling his hair.

Moments later Sandra reluctantly released herself from Karl's embracing arms and blushed a little as she realized that she smelled of sex.

"Would it be alright if I grab a quick shower?"

"Yes, by all means. The bathroom is the second door on the right. There are plenty of clean towels hanging on the rail."

"Thank you," said Sandra, half-smiling as her hand touched his cheek with affection. She bent down to kiss him gently on the lips and as she drew herself back up she noted that his expression was warm and grateful.

Sandra departed, eager to freshen herself up.

Slipping out of her clothes she turned on the shower taps and adjusted the setting, before stepping into the shower enclosure.

The jets of water cascaded down her body, massaging her form like a million tiny fingers. It was pure luxury and at that precise moment she could think of nothing more relaxing. Soaping herself down, she watched as the lather was rinsed from her body to swirl down into the plughole's mini whirlpool.

As the last of the suds disappeared she shut off the taps and stepped out of the shower cubicle. As droplets of water peppered the carpet she wrapped herself in one of the fluffy white woollen bath towels and patted herself dry.

She did not bother to get dressed again, choosing instead to stay wrapped within the soft warm fluffy towel.

Opening the bathroom door she padded back into the living room to see their half empty wine glasses sat upon the coffee table, the dent in the armchair indicating where Karl had been sitting.

Candles had been lit and music filtered gently through the room.

As she glanced around, Karl appeared with the already opened bottle of rich red wine from the kitchen and proceeded to top up their glasses.

"Did you enjoy your shower?"

"Yes thanks. I am feeling much better now."

Her voice was coloured with arousal.

Noting the decline into night, Karl went over to the curtains and drew them tight.

Karl then approached Sandra and took her in his arms, the momentum almost sweeping her off her feet as he released the towel that was covering her modesty.

Sandra thought that he was going to kiss her but he committed only with his hands, which journeyed slowly across the contours of her flesh, climbing the gentle mounds of her small firm breasts, lingering at her hardened nipples before exploring the flatlands of her firm abdomen and probing the partially shaven depths of her once blonde valley. Sandra obligingly spread her thighs allowing Karl's fingers to continue their progress into the increasingly moist cavern contained there. His thumb nuzzled the throbbing bud, exposed like a pearl in an oyster shell. He lay her down on the settee and she propped herself up on the cushions to study the motion of Karl's hand between her legs, as his fingers curled and dived into her temple of love. As the pleasure intensified she lay back and enjoyed the slow rhythmic, almost hypnotic, movement. Closing her eyes, she drifted into erotic sexual reverie. Welcoming the pleasure, her nipples tightened with desire, standing taut.

Karl hoped that he had found a new reason for living…

A few moments later, Sandra returned to full wakefulness as Karl's fingers had ceased their delicate investigations and now rested unmoving inside her.

She looked up, raising her head, and received a deep and lengthy kiss.

Karl's eyes were alight with desire as a smile lit up his face like a beacon.

Removing his fingers he proceeded to slide his rod into her moist lips and glided in and out in a slow patient rhythm. Sandra moaned, wriggling as she thrust herself into Karl's groin, eager to take every inch of him. Raw animal lust overtook them as the intensity of their desire grew ever stronger. Feeling her bud throbbing under the increasing pressure, she moaned with an involuntary spasm. They came together with a tremor, Sandra's moans of ecstasy only being drowned out by Karl's shuddering cry as he ejaculated inside her.

Opening their eyes and gasping for breath, they eased themselves apart and slid from the settee. Karl's fingers were still so wet that he had to dry them on some tissues from the box that sat upon the coffee table for just such emergencies…well that, and the Baywatch re-runs…

It had been so long since he had been touched with affection and he felt happier than ever before. Sandra had lifted his spirits and his guilt had begun to recede, to be replaced by warm memories of their first and now most recent meetings…the intimacy that followed and the delightful anticipation of more to come. In his mind's eye he mentally pushed his emotional baggage to one side as something about Sandra made him feel nice, reassured, comforted, familiar…

It still felt strange to have someone genuinely care about him after all those years of parental indifference and meaningless and sordid one night stands. It was not usual for him to find glamour in the usual mundane sordidness.

He had never experienced love before…everything was changed, although deep down he knew that Sandra would never grant him absolution and that in itself would open up a whole new arena of guilt.

Although these new developments had not fully terminated his desire to kill, it had, for the moment, seriously curtailed it.

Karl's face set a little; he tugged at his earlobe.

He yearned for a fresh start without the coiled anger and hurt of the past.

Whereas previously he saw only terror and a flat, endless plain of emptiness ahead of him, now he had hope, albeit slight.

His heart leapt at the possibility – Sandra's precious words of comfort were swallowed whole, but alas he still needed some way to absorb the guilt that he now felt.

As Sandra wrapped the towel around her body, he slipped his arm around her waist and guided her into the bedroom. Karl strolled over to the curtains and drew them tight. As he undressed, he felt pleasantly tired. Sleepily contented they climbed into the bed, lowering themselves into the dark, as Karl switched off the bedside light. The bedroom window was left slightly ajar, the cool breeze soon lulling them to a contented sleep in each other's arms.

CHAPTER 16

THE RAID

The murder squad now knew the murderer's identity and the twisted details of his life, but still a nagging doubt teased at the back of their minds.

Detective Inspector Ross, who had just returned from a meeting with the Police Commissioner, entered the squad room.

As he gave the final briefing to his team, he hoped that his voice carried the required authority as inside he felt sick and almost out of breath. As he spoke his face animated and reddened as inwardly his nerves buzzed. His mouth had gone dry and he felt almost close to tears. He began to take slow regular breaths in a bid to remain calm, but not wanting to disrupt his train of thought.

A uniformed police officer poked his head round the door and without uttering a word placed a mug of coffee down on Detective Inspector Ross's table.

Detective Inspector Ross nodded an acknowledgement.

He momentarily paused to take a sip of the coffee before continuing with the fresh flow of words, jumping into the plan of action.

A firearms team was to be deployed to the home address.

The trick now was to get to the target's location quickly without the suspect becoming aware or being tipped off.

He glanced across at Detective Sergeant Armstrong who was dressed in a dark sports jacket and grey flannel trousers.

He looked set for a day on the golf course as opposed to a dawn raid, but he let the observation go unvoiced as he had more pressing issues at present.

They were quickly approaching the moment of truth and that always made him slightly nervous. He took the arrest and search warrants and folded them in half to slip into his inside jacket pocket, for safekeeping.

Detective Sergeant Armstrong had met Detective Inspector Ross's eyes but gave no indication of his approval or disapproval in regards to the intended course of action. If the shit hit the fan over this one, he wanted to have maintained a fence sitting position. That way he could jump on whichever side best suited his needs. He liked to think of it as his Prescott position…

He wondered where Detective Sergeant Ryder had got to. Although she was only in on the investigation at the death and had the last few days booked off months ago, he would have thought that she would have rescheduled them under the circumstances. Numerous phone messages had been left on both her home and mobile phones but as yet no contact with her had been made.

Maybe she had just decided to go away for a few days and left the phone at home to free herself from the pull and burden of work?

He just hoped that she was alright…

*   *   *

Traffic was light due to the ungodly hour, so they soon arrived at the target's address. They cut the engine and switched off the lights.

Detective Sergeant Armstrong, who was sat in the passenger seat, reached back into the rear seat of the car to retrieve a plastic carrier bag. From it he produced a Thermos flask containing coffee and a spare plastic mug. Filling it, he offered it to Detective Inspector Ross.

"No, you are alright mate. I will be bursting for a pee otherwise."

Detective Sergeant Armstrong nodded absently before he took a few sips of the steaming liquid, reluctantly throwing the remainder out onto the pavement as he could see that Detective Inspector Ross was keen to get cracking.

The street was dark and deserted, the moon high above illuminating the clear night sky.

A breeze whipped down the avenue, rustling the trees and tugging at the leaves on the branches.

The road was devoid of movement except for the partially concealed officers skulking in the shadows.

A lone tabby cat sat drinking from a puddle, blissfully unaware of the mayhem that was about to ensue…or more likely just not caring.

The scene had been secured and was currently being protected by the armed response unit.

Detective Inspector Ross had taken control of the scene soon after his arrival and was currently preparing himself for the raid.

The suspect's car sat in the driveway, whilst the one story house (which reeked of elegance and money) remained unilluminated.

Detective Inspector Ross scanned the windows of the house once more, but every one was concealed with darkness, none of the closed curtains were twitching so the house seemed as quiet as a grave.

If they had not known better, it would have appeared to them as if no one was at home.

Thankfully the target had been observed drawing, what they assumed to be, the bedroom curtains a short time ago, so they knew that Karl was at home. Alas, whether he was alone was still very much uncertain.

For a moment Detective Sergeant Armstrong and Detective Inspector Ross stood in silence, wrapped up in the shroud of nervous anticipation.

A police van pulled up and more armed officers equipped with bullet proof vests, guns, helmets and battering rams scrambled out. Keeping the headlights low a similar vehicle arrived from the other direction and its personnel did likewise.

Unmarked police cars sat on the other side of the road, a few hundred yards down.

The sound of a car on an adjacent road echoed down the street and then died away, so that peace reigned once more.

Harsh stark moonlight shone down on the officers as they prepared themselves to enter the targeted premises.

Sparks of electric tension filled the air but no one spoke as the respective watches were checked …

They were due to enter the property at four AM.

A heavy silence fell between them until one of the uniformed officers, with the standard police battering ram in hand, moved towards the solid wooden door.

The air felt fresh and damp upon their faces.

As the officers passed through the gate and proceeded up the driveway, the sensor lights picked up their less than stealthy movements and beamed a response, illuminating the driveway in a bright fluorescent golden glow.

Detective Inspector Ross seeing the element of surprise slip away bit his lip in frustration, whilst a small 'v' knitted his eyebrows together, momentarily deepening his already well defined facial wrinkles.

He clenched his fist and stamped his feet in anger.

"Shit. Let's get a move on here."

The police officer carrying the solo battering ram in his hands, charged at the hinged barrier. The officer hit the door hard with the ram; the door creaked almost painfully, but did not budge.

Detective Inspector Ross cast a glance of contempt.

The police officer knowing that time was of the essence quickly took aim with the ram for a second time adding weight to the contact. As the impact was made the door yielded and wood splinters flew everywhere as the lock smashed under the force of the assault. The door was then kicked fully open.

The armed officers took the lead and dived into the residence as if they were attack dogs. The adrenaline was now coursing through their veins, their machismo awaiting deployment.

Karl, startled from his previous slumber, awoke to hear the sound of his front door crash open, an explosion of wood sent splintering into the wall. Karl could barely focus as he squinted at the digital alarm clock that sat perched upon his bedside cabinet – it stated that it was 4:01am.

He turned his attention towards the bedroom doorway, eyes wide, seized by an alarming hysteria. His hand slipped beneath his pillows to grasp his hunting knife, as he threw back the bed covers from his body.

Sandra, who had also been roused from her sleep, was unaware of what was taking place - for the moment too much red wine had taken its toll on her reasoning, but in truth nothing could have prepared her for a fate as barbarous and unnatural as the one about to befall her. She listened to Karl's breathing, each deep inhalation and exhalation heavy with blame, the wordless air of reproach.

At that moment the bedroom door crashed open, rocking on its hinges, the noise reverberating like a kettledrum.

Shadowy figures emerged, their black silhouettes half framed in the doorway. The officers proceeded to shout a jumbled mixture of threats and instructions.

Sandra shook, not a great movement, slight and contained, but containing an enormous mixture of rage and fear.

Karl, who was breathing heavily, was momentarily frozen, uncertain of what to do, so it was Sandra who spoke first.

"Just what the hell is going on here?"

Before a response could be given she spotted Detective Inspector Ross in the doorway. He recognized Sandra in the same instant, shock settling upon both their faces before they had time to conceal it.

Karl frowned at her quizzically; eventually Sandra looked sideways and met his eyes.

Unfortunately Karl had caught the look of recognition between them. He closed his eyes for a brief moment as if hoping to then awake from a dream, but that only began a sickening dizziness that spun him round as if he trapped upon a fairground ride. Darting across his fear and suspense a sharp shiver shook him suddenly and rattled his teeth as the implication of it all sank in. Karl blinked at her; the idea was so clearly rooted in his mind that it took a moment for reality to adjust itself.

Karl said nothing. He wasn't thinking about himself, or the cold goose pimples of realization rising up on his flesh, or even Sandra, who was shaking and jabbering incoherently by his side, but about the utter futility of life.

A heavy silence then fell between them as Sandra began to struggle into a sitting position, her face drained of colour.

Karl, sensing the betrayal, grabbed her by the arm as he brought the hunting knife up to hover menacingly at her throat.

Detective Inspector Armstrong stood looking on incredulous.

As Karl turned his head to look into Sandra's eyes he saw only trepidation and a flat, endless plain of desolation; their 'moment' together had gone.

The joy and hope that he had previously felt was to be replaced by the betrayal that had haunted him throughout his life, but instead of sadness he felt a terrible rage.

Now it was Sandra's turn to momentarily freeze as if startled by a dream-memory, either unsure of what was going on, or just not wanting to believe the realization that was now beginning to dawn on her.

The new development led the advancing officers to freeze in their tracks.

"Put the knife down."

It was Detective Inspector Ross who had shouted out the instruction, suddenly fearing for the immediate safety of one of his own team.

There would now be enough tricky and embarrassing questions to be answered without losing one of their own officers.

Armed police officers inched forward, circling the bed from either side.

"Stay back or I will kill her."

Karl's throat was dry and his voice crackled from the combination of the distress and its disuse.

The glance of disgust from Detective Inspector Ross passed over him but left him unscathed as his own mind was already inflicting the fatal wounds as a cyclone of grief, anger and frustration whirled inside of him. His only chance of a normal life had now been stolen from him. His mind clung to the last faint shreds of lucidity as his world, haunted by darkness and terror slowly turned black. The wounds in his heart would now never be healed. His only true love had turned out to be a police officer, but he doubted that he would have time to contemplate life's little ironies at any great length.

Still seething with a sense of injustice and treachery, Karl felt that there was indeed a hateful wrongness with the world beyond the mere mechanical cruelty of it all.

The silence that had followed seemed like the heaviest and longest enduring that he had known in that house, but just then a cool breeze purred at the windows as the sound of a car echoed up from the road outside before dying away.

As Karl turned his head towards Sandra he noted how pale and frail she now looked, even her eyes seemed to have lost some of their colour and enchantment. She looked cold and was shaking, unable to speak or look away from him, her eyes peering fearfully at him. He felt a momentary lapse in anger but remained gripping her with the knife still trained menacingly at her throat. Karl's unwavering stare seemed to cause Sandra a power backflow, draining her of energy and confidence, her police training now completely forgotten. Yet still she could not seem to drag her eyes away, his mastery seemingly holding her spellbound.

Her hunched shoulders began to shake as she started to cry. Sandra began to try to speak but her muffled words were to be drowned out.

"We are armed police. Put the knife down and you won't get hurt."

Karl could not help but to wonder if similar words had been uttered to the Brazilian Jean Charles de Menezes shortly before he had become the latest victim of a state-sanctioned murder.

A silence had set in – a deep silence before Sandra again tried to speak, but coloured by a grey wash of despair her voice had grown thinner as she attempted to orate. Her voice, wracked by sobs, was little above a whisper.

"No, please he will…"

That was all she could say before collapsing into tears.

Once again the armed officer's warning rang out menacingly, cutting off her words as she attempted to get her intended message across.

"This is your final warning – drop your weapon to the floor, now!"

Just as the sentence hung unanswered in the air, Karl heard a shot ring out.

He gritted his teeth in almost unbearable pain as his body lurched sideways, to be thrown against Sandra's. A scorching pain seared his chest as floating images ran through his mind. Although he was weakened by the impact of the bullet the knife however remained tightly in his grasp, as did Sandra. Karl groaned in pain, gasping for breath, gagging on blood and splitting out red saliva.

Just then a second shot rang out. He opened his mouth to scream in pain but only a soft gargling sound escaped from his throat. He thought that he was going to pass out from the pain that flashed like a lightning strike all the way through his body. Blood oozed from the wounds on his body as his vision blurred. He turned to Sandra, who was now screaming hysterically as tears filled her eyes, touched suddenly by a different sadness.

"I am so very sorry."

His words were soaked in blood, whilst his fingers released his grip on the knife, his eyes reproachful.

"Go", Karl urged her in a croaking whisper, his voice sounding thin and stretched.

At that precise moment he cried out in agony as a third bullet staggered him, the sharp burst of pain toppling him from the bed face down onto the deep pile carpet, bringing up clouds of pale dust that choked him. The knife slipped from his grasp and he felt himself being pounced upon by a mass of heavy bodies.

Blood oozed from his wounds, soaking into the carpet.

He felt himself becoming weaker as his life force drained away, but he wanted to feel the pain, as it was all he had left. Life was never the answer; he just hoped that death would now solve the riddle. He knew that he was not yet dead but he sensed that he was not alive either, stuck somewhere in-between, as if halfway on a journey. He could not see if any other worlds were waiting beyond the one that he currently inhabited but for a moment he lay still, trembling, eyes closed until the truth revealed itself and his world turned black.

Detective Inspector Ross had walked back across to the bed and was now cradling Sandra in his arms. Her once blonde hair was now caked in blood and hanging down in rats' tails across her shoulders. Her body was still shaking, her pallor ghostly, her voice not yet returned.

She began to ease herself gently up into a fully upright sitting position but with the difficulty of an old woman.

Detective Inspector Ross still held her, wanting to comfort and protect her, but his need to know proved too much to keep within.

"Are you alright? Did he rape you?"

Sandra was unable to answer the questions as her eyes once again filled up with tears and sobs wracked her body, her emotions flowing out of control, a mixture of sadness and gratitude.

Tears welled up in Detective Inspector Ross's eyes as rage filled him with a burning tremulous heat. Taking Sandra's silence as confirmation of abduction and sexual assault revenge raged within him. The power of rational thought had temporarily left him whilst the overwhelming anger poured in. Possible consequences were momentarily forgotten, wisdom cast aside to the winds of revenge.

With eyes blazing he climbed off the bed and turned, swinging his leg around to lash a hefty kick into the ribs of Karl's prone body. Detective Sergeant Armstrong pulled him away before he could land the second one.

Karl was dead and his pain was long gone but for his victims' families their suffering would long continue.

As the clamour of sirens echoed through the previously deserted streets Detective Inspector Ross returned to the bed and cradled Sandra in his arms as he waited for the ambulance to arrive. Her clothes and hair were soaked with blood. She remained speechless as she lifted her hands up to sob through her fingers. A thin smear of blood trailed across her face like the slime from a snail, currently adding the only touch of colour to her ghostly appearance.

Still unable to speak, her face, though streaked with tears, was etched with disbelief, her heart crushed. She felt feeble, shaky, gasping…

Although the task had now been completed, strangely the acts of retribution and vengeance had brought Detective Inspector Ross no relief from his pain, no personal sense of triumph.

The room had gone momentarily silent and Detective Inspector Ross could sense the assembled officers' eyes fixed inscrutably upon him.

He felt the tears of self-pity that had been reluctantly gathering in his eyes begin to fall, to be soaked up by the duvet beneath him.

He could not honestly say that he regretted what they had done as the shooting had been a payback and their own brand of justice in honour of all the grieving families that the murderous scumbag had left behind.

Summoning up every reserve of strength that he had – or so it felt – he steeled himself for the arrival of the paramedics and the police back-up units.

He felt frustrated, his sense of fate and direction subverted by the recent events.

Around him light switches were being turned on, their corresponding bulbs now burning his eyes, momentarily leaving a ghostly image of naked light bulbs that drifted across his field of vision.

He wondered how much his life had changed as he viewed his mental re-creations. As his mind played him pictures he continued to hold Sandra, her quivering body moulding into his as a heavy blanket of depression covered them both.

Sandra's destiny and his were momentarily entwined as he spoke what he hoped to be comforting words.

"Just hang on in there. It is all over now. He cannot hurt you anymore. The ambulance will be here very shortly. You will be alright, trust me."

Sandra held his gaze for a second before she nodded, albeit a little queasily, but with her previously tear stained vision now clearing through the shallow pool of tears.

Detective Inspector Ross continued to comfort her as he considered the situation for a moment briefly embarrassed but unsure whether it was for himself or Sandra…or the both of them.

His composure trembled and he barely managed to keep the mask of assurance firmly in place.

Sandra was in shock and as such was mentally removed from the current situation and removed from herself. She was now a woman who events had pushed through and then beyond the normal play of emotions, to a deadened place.

EPILOGUE

As the crime scene was being cordoned off and a search of the property undertaken Detective Inspector Ross sat alone in his car. An element of resignation filtered through him as he realized that from now on his life would operate from the baseline of despair. His stomach filled with lead at the thought whilst his throat felt dry and his body drained of energy. He shook his head slowly as a weary resignation had engulfed his body, his emotions flowing out of control as tears cascaded down his cheeks. His face was coloured by a grey wash of despair, compounded by the realization that his adversaries were always going to be brutal and relentless. They would be men who were so removed from civilized behaviour and beyond the normal play of emotions, that they resided in the numbest place.

Much as he loved the memory of life he had no option but to accept it.

He momentarily closed his eyes before opening them again hoping to prove that it had all been a bad dream…it was not.

He could no longer find the energy to be aggressive. He heard the voices of police officers stood nearby but he was not really listening, he was wondering what life now held for him.

Feeling stiff and robotic as a small battle raged within him, his instincts fighting back against the weight of his depression. After the recent events he now had a clearer sense of what was missing from his life but at present no idea of how to get it back. The investigation had called into question many of Detective Inspector Ross's previous assumptions about the manner in which people behaved, including himself.

He now realised that damaged children grew up in different ways and whereas some could shrug off the perturbation of their past, others could not change who they were or what they had become.

Unfortunately due to the social and political climate and the breakdown of family values the unyielding fact was that there were always going to be people spawning more Karl Connors…